"It's never going to work. Why can't you accept that?"

"Because I'm nothing but a spoiled rich girl used to getting her own way."

"Even spoiled rich girls have to learn to accept defeat."

"Damn you, Ethan Stormwalker…. Tell me you don't care." She took a step toward him. "Tell me that I don't mean anything to you, that you haven't missed me as much as I've missed you." Another step. "Tell me I'm not the reason you're out here, unable to sleep."

"Dammit, Cindy…"

"Tell me, Ethan, and I'll go away and you'll never have to see me again."

She was close. Too close. And he wanted her more than he wanted to see another sunrise.

Dear Reader,

In the spirit of Valentine's Day, we have some wonderful stories for you this February from Silhouette Romance to guarantee that every day is filled with love and tenderness.

DeAnna Talcott puts a fresh spin on the tale of Cupid, who finally meets her match in *Cupid Jones Gets Married* (#1646), the latest in the popular SOULMATES series. And Carla Cassidy has been working overtime with her incredibly innovative, incredibly fun duo, *What if I'm Pregnant...?* (#1644) and *If the Stick Turns Pink...* (#1645), about the promise of love a baby could bring to two special couples!

Then Elizabeth Harbison takes us on a fairy-tale adventure in *Princess Takes a Holiday* (#1643). A glamour-weary royal who hides her identity meets the man of her dreams when her car breaks down in a small North Carolina town. In *Dude Ranch Bride* (#1642), Madeline Baker brings us strong, sexy Lakota Ethan Stormwalker, whose ex-flame shows up at his ranch in a wedding gown—without a groom! And in Donna Clayton's *Thunder in the Night* (#1647), the third in THE THUNDER CLAN family saga, a single act of kindness changes Conner Thunder's life forever....

Be sure to come back next month for more emotion-filled love stories from Silhouette Romance. Happy reading!

Mary-Theresa Hussey

Mary-Theresa Hussey
Senior Editor

Please address questions and book requests to:
Silhouette Reader Service
U.S.: 3010 Walden Ave., P.O. Box 1325, Buffalo, NY 14269
Canadian: P.O. Box 609, Fort Erie, Ont. L2A 5X3

Madeline Baker

DUDE RANCH BRIDE

SILHOUETTE *Romance*®

Published by Silhouette Books

America's Publisher of Contemporary Romance

This book is dedicated to

Lisa Kelley, Carol Holko, Ronda Thompson, Karen Morriss,
Kay Coulter, Tanya Dickson, Laura Shinn,
Beverly Gladstone, Jean Paquin, Kurt Boze,
Mike Townsend and Don (I hope I haven't forgotten anyone!)

for adding to my Star Wars collection.
May the Force be with you…always!

 SILHOUETTE BOOKS

ISBN 0-373-19642-3

DUDE RANCH BRIDE

Printed in U.S.A.

Anymore.

I hardly think of him at all
except for summer, winter, spring and fall
or when someone else says his name
or I feel the heat of a candle's flame
or hear a certain country song
about a love that done gone wrong.

And now, so it seems
he's hardly ever in my dreams
and I hardly cry anymore at all
except for summer, winter, spring and fall
and if I sometimes call his name
who can say that I'm to blame
when his memory haunts me still
but then, I guess it always will.

—Cindy Wagner
August 19, 1998

Chapter One

Cindy Wagner clutched her father's arm in a death grip as they walked down the aisle toward the altar. She couldn't go through with this. Why had she let it go this far?

Her father reached over and patted her hand. "Relax," he whispered.

Relax? How on earth could she relax? She glanced at the long white runner that stretched ahead of her, at the pretty white satin bows at the end of the pews, the tall white wicker holders filled with fresh pink and white rosebuds and baby's breath. Her maid of honor and five bridesmaids, all dressed in shades of mauve and carrying bouquets of pink carnations, stood there looking far happier than she felt, no doubt remembering their own weddings or dreaming of ones to come. Cindy's two brothers, Lance and Joe, stood beside Paul, together with Paul's two brothers and his cousin.

Why had she let her father talk her into this marriage?

From the corner of her eye, she saw her mother sitting in the front row, looking proud and sad at the same time.

Her father winced as she dug her fingernails into his arm.

Another few steps and they were at the altar. The scent of roses filled the air.

Her dad leaned over and kissed her cheek and then placed her hand, her cold trembling hand, into Paul's. Feeling abandoned, Cindy sent a mute appeal to her father, who smiled reassuringly and took a step backward. With a sigh of resignation, she turned to face the minister.

"Marriage is an honorable estate," the pastor began, "and not to be entered into lightly...."

She slid a furtive glance toward Paul. He was tall and blond and handsome, with light brown eyes and a fine straight nose. He was ambitious, even-tempered and even richer than her father. But did she want to spend the rest of her life with him? Cindy tried to tell herself that her doubts were caused by nothing more than last minute jitters—very last minute jitters, to be sure. But she knew her uncertainty went far deeper than just a case of nerves. Paul wanted to be in the limelight. He had high ambitions and saw himself running for public office in a year or two, but it wasn't the kind of life she wanted. All she wanted to do was get married and raise three or four happy, healthy children with a man who would put his wife and children first.

Paul had made her forget that for a while. He had swept her off her feet, wined her and dined her in all the best restaurants in town, showered her with flowers and candy. Caught up in the whirlwind that was Paul VanDerHyde, she had let him convince her that she loved him.

Why hadn't she listened to her mother?

"He'll never make you happy, honey," Claire Wagner had told her not twenty minutes ago. "It's not too late to change your mind."

"Mom, are you crazy?" Cindy had met her gaze in the mirror as her mother pinned her veil in place.

Not too late? There was a mountain of wedding gifts back at the house, a stretch limo waiting to take them to the airport. The bridal suite at The Plaza in New York City was reserved for them. She sighed. She hadn't wanted to go to New York on her honeymoon, but Paul had swept away her objections, saying they would have a wonderful time, assuring her that his business there would only take one day, two at the most. They could go to Hawaii some other time.

The minister's voice brought her back to the here and now. "And do you, Cynthia Elizabeth Wagner, take Paul Raymond VanDerHyde…"

Her mouth was dry, her palms damp. She heard her mother's voice in the back of her mind: *Do you love him so much you can't imagine life without him?* And Cindy knew the answer was no.

She looked at Paul and, for one wild moment, it was another face she saw. A strong masculine face framed by long black hair. And that, she thought, was the real reason she couldn't go through with this wedding. Not now. Not ever. There was only one man she couldn't imagine living without, and it wasn't Paul VanDerHyde.

Overcome by a sudden sense of panic, she tugged on Paul's hand to get his attention. "I can't do this," she whispered. "I'm sorry."

She almost tripped on the hem of her dress as she freed her hand from his, then turned and ran down the aisle as fast as her high heels would permit, her veil billowing behind her. How could she have let Paul's money, his romantic endearments, the large engagement ring, outweigh her doubts and cloud her judgment? How had she ever thought to find happiness with Paul when she was marrying him more to please her father than herself?

She ran faster, her eyes blurred by her tears, a sob building in her throat as she rounded the corner, pushed through the big double doors and hurried down the stairs toward the waiting limo.

The driver opened the rear door for her. Holding her veil with one hand, she ducked into the back seat.

"Go!" she said. "Now. Go. Hurry!"

The driver nodded, as if runaway brides were an everyday occurrence in his line of work. Sliding behind the wheel, he turned the key in the ignition just as Paul and members of the wedding party burst through the doorway.

"Where to?" the driver asked.

"I don't know." She sank back against the butter-soft leather seat. "Just drive."

"Yes, ma'am," he said, and pulled onto the street.

She stared out the window, watching the scenery pass by in a blur of tears. Where did runaway brides go? Where could she hide where no one would find her? A place where she wouldn't have to explain what she had done or why. Some place where no one would know who she was.

They had been driving for several hours when she saw the billboard on the side of the road. Leaning forward, she read:

Elk Valley Dude Ranch 15 miles ahead.
Hunting. Fishing. Horseback riding.
Cabins with or without cooking facilities.
Available by the Day, Week, or Month.
Reasonable Rates.

Elk Valley Dude Ranch. Just reading the words sent unwanted frissons of excitement running through her.

Cindy closed her eyes, wondering if going there would be wise. She knew no one would look for her at a dude ranch, but there was always a chance *he* might show up there. For the last five years, every time she had seen a tall, broad-shouldered man with long black hair, her heart had skipped a beat in anticipation.

She hoped he *would* be there. Seeing him again might be a good thing, she decided, wiping the last of her tears from her eyes. Maybe confronting him again would banish him from her heart once and for all.

Chapter Two

Ethan Stormwalker swore under his breath as a long white limo pulled up in front of the ranch office. Man, Dorothea must be expecting some mighty rich greenhorns this time, he mused with a shake of his head. Most guests arrived at the ranch in dusty vans or SUVs, or driving old station wagons.

The limo driver exited the vehicle, straightened his jacket and opened the back door. Ethan nearly fell down the stairs as a woman clad in a long white wedding gown stepped out of the car. He couldn't help staring. Her hair, piled in thick curls atop her head, was as black as his own. She had lovely clear skin, generous curves in all the right places, and a waist so small he could span it with his hands. At this distance, he couldn't see her eyes, but he knew they were as clear and blue as the Montana sky overhead.

He whistled softly. He hadn't seen her in five years, but he had carried her image in his mind and in his heart every day of those years. She had always been a knockout, and he swore again, envying the guy that had been lucky enough to marry her. Ethan waited, curious to see what kind of man Cynthia Elizabeth Wagner had picked.

Cindy spoke to the driver, then lifted her skirts to keep them out of the dirt as she walked toward the office, her veil blowing lightly in the breeze.

Ethan quickly turned his back, pretending to study the notices thumbtacked to the bulletin board. What the hell was she doing here, and how was he going to avoid her? He glanced back at the limo, wondering where the groom was. He couldn't see anything or anyone through the tinted windows.

The bell above the door chimed softly as she opened it and stepped inside. He told himself to get out of there before she came back out, but he didn't move, only stood there like some nerdy high school kid hoping to catch a glimpse of the prom queen.

She emerged from the office a few moments later. From the corner of his eye, Ethan watched her descend the stairs. She spoke to the driver, who went around the back of the limo, opened the trunk and lifted out a small overnight case and a black handbag. He handed both to Cindy, smiled at her, then slid behind the wheel of the limo and drove off.

She stood there a moment, staring after the limo, a wistful expression on her face, and then marched across the yard and back into the office.

No groom? Consumed with curiosity, Ethan was tempted to follow her inside, but he'd just got back from a long trail ride with eleven city kids and he needed a hot shower and a cold beer, in that order. And he had vowed never to speak to Cindy Wagner again, not in this life and not in the next.

With a shake of his head, he shoved her out of his mind and headed for the corral.

Cindy tossed her overnight case and purse on the cabin's double bed, along with the bag of new clothes she had just bought at the gift shop. Then, with a sigh, she sat down on the foot of the bed.

She glanced around the room. Though the outside of the cabin was made of rough-hewn logs, the interior seemed modern enough. There was a double bed, a dresser and mirror, a comfy looking, overstuffed chair, a couple of tables with Western-style lamps, and a TV set. She could see a sink and small refrigerator in the next room.

She looked at the bag on the bed and thought of the two suitcases filled with her trousseau waiting for her at the hotel where they had booked the reception, and the slinky, ice-blue silk suit that was to have been her going away outfit. And the frothy white negligee she had planned to wear later tonight. And the gauzy black one. And the silky red one… Oh, well, there was no help for it now. Her mother would get her things and they would be waiting for her when she got home, though she didn't know if she would ever want to wear anything that would remind her of today's fiasco.

For a moment, Cindy stared at the colorful throw rug on the floor. Her life was like that, she thought, a lot of colors woven together with no visible pattern. What was she going to tell her parents? What was she going to tell Paul? How would she ever face her friends and family again? Her brothers would never let her hear the end of it, especially Lance. Why had she ever let things go so far?

With a shake of her head, she kicked off her white satin pumps. Judging by the look of surprise on the face of the woman Cindy had talked to in the office, she was the first person to ever show up at the dude ranch wearing a wedding dress, or at least the first bride to show up without a groom at her side. Cindy was lucky there had been a last minute cancellation.

She stepped out of her lacy white half slip and draped it over the back of the chair in the corner.

It was no easy task, unfastening the long row of tiny,

silk-covered buttons that ran down the back of her dress, but she finally managed it. It was a beautiful gown, she thought as she spread it over the petticoat, exactly the kind of dress she had always dreamed of being married in. Unpinning her veil, she laid it on top of her gown.

She stared at the ring on her finger, felt the sting of tears in her eyes as she took it off and placed it inside her overnight case. How could she have let things go so far? Why had she let Paul make all their decisions? He had decided when they would get married, had picked out the church, had decided where they would have the reception, where they would go for their honeymoon. The worst of it was, he had convinced her that she wanted a huge wedding, a huge reception and a honeymoon in New York City, when what she had really wanted was a small wedding and a honeymoon in Hawaii.

She pulled off the pretty white garter with its tiny, pink satin flowers and dropped it into her overnight case, then peeled off her panty hose and tossed them on top of the dress. Pulling the pins from her curls, she shook her head until her hair fell down around her shoulders. That was another thing. She had wanted to wear her hair down, but Paul liked it up.

It infuriated her, to think how he had manipulated her! How she had let him get away with it! She was a smart woman. She had a B.A. in nineteenth-century American history and a mind of her own, yet Paul VanDerHyde had breezed into her life and taken it over as if he had every right to do so. And she had let him! Never again! She was through with arrogant macho men. Maybe through with men altogether! Her aunt Stell seemed perfectly happy living alone with her eight cats, three dogs and a parrot that quoted Sylvester Stallone movies....

Cindy laughed in spite of herself as she tugged on the jeans she had bought. So maybe she wasn't ready to become a recluse surrounded by pets. But it would be a long time before she looked twice at any man again unless he had Russell Crowe's sexy voice, eyes like Antonio Banderas, Mel Gibson's smile, a body like a Greek god. And long black hair like...

She shook his image and his name from her mind. She had once vowed never to think of him again, yet she seemed to see him at every turn. Even the man she had seen standing outside the office had reminded her of him, but maybe that was to be expected, since a member of his family owned the ranch. She never should have come here!

"Get over it!" she muttered. "I'm sure he has."

She pulled a blue T-shirt emblazoned with the Elk Valley Dude Ranch logo from the sack and slipped it over her head. The woman in the office had told her there was a town a few miles away where she could buy more than just jeans and souvenir T-shirts. Her nephew went in every Monday for supplies, the woman had said; Cindy was welcome to go along with him if she was so inclined.

The only shoes available at the gift shop had been a pair of plastic sandals with huge, hot pink, plastic roses on top. Slipping them on, she decided to go outside and have a look around. Sooner or later, she would have to call home and let her parents know she was all right, but not now. For now, all she wanted was to be alone in her misery.

Tucking the key to her cabin into the pocket of her jeans, she stepped outside, locking the door behind her.

There seemed to be people everywhere—hanging over the corral fence watching a cowboy ride a bronc, playing horseshoes and shuffleboard and volleyball, or just sitting in the shade or relaxing in the late afternoon sun.

Cindy wasn't in the mood to be with people or indulge in aimless chitchat, or, worse yet, explain what she was doing there alone. Going around the back of her cabin, she spied a narrow trail that led away from the ranch yard.

The scenery was lovely, and for a moment she forgot everything else. Caught up in the natural beauty around her, she followed the dirt path. It ran alongside a shallow, winding stream lined by tall trees whose silvery leaves whispered in the soft summer breeze.

As she rounded a bend in the trail, another cabin came into view. A dog that looked more like a wolf was stretched out on the porch. It lifted its head and stared at her through large amber eyes, and Cindy noticed its sharp white teeth. *The better to eat you with, my dear,* she thought.

A large buckskin horse paced back and forth in a peeled-pole corral, pausing now and then to paw the ground or shake its head. She didn't know much about horses other than what little she recalled from the riding lessons she'd had years ago, but this one was beautiful. Its coat gleamed like burnished gold, its mane and tail looked like black silk. It snorted and laid its ears back as she approached the corral.

"Hey! Get away from there!"

Cindy whirled around and felt the color drain from her face as she saw a man clad in nothing but a pair of faded blue jeans and a pair of moccasins stride toward her from the far side of the cabin. Tall and lean and broad-shouldered, he had long black hair, high cheekbones, a strong jaw, a hawklike nose. His skin was a smooth copper color all over, just as she remembered. She almost sighed as he shrugged on a faded blue shirt, leaving it unbuttoned.

"You! What are you doing here?" she exclaimed. And then wondered why she was so surprised. She'd known someone in his family owned the ranch. Deep down, hadn't she come here hoping to see him?

He stared at her. His eyes were the color of gray storm clouds, dark and angry.

"What the hell are *you* doing here?" he asked brusquely.

"I asked you first."

"I work here."

"Well, I didn't know that."

He grunted softly. He was sure of that. She never would have come if she had known he was here.

She couldn't stop looking at him. He had been handsome at nineteen; now, five years later, the promise of youth had been fulfilled. He had an arresting face, all sharp planes and angles that, taken separately, should have been ordinary. But there was nothing ordinary about this man's face. Or his body. Heat flowed through her. She had a sudden urge to run her hands over that broad chest to see if it was as hard and firm as she remembered, to feel his sun-warmed skin beneath her fingertips. His jeans fit his long, long legs like a second skin.

"Seen enough," he drawled insolently, "or should I strip down to my shorts?"

Ethan grinned when she blushed and looked away. He should be used to those looks by now, he thought. He had been propositioned more times than he could count in the last two years. Lonely women, unhappily married women, teenage girls, rich society babes like Cindy Wagner—he seemed to attract them all. But Cindy was the only woman who had ever captured his heart. Captured it and refused to let it go, even when she no longer wanted it.

"I...I'm, that is...it was nice seeing you again, Ethan. I should be going," she stammered. Head lowered, she swept past him.

He turned to watch her. She looked good walking away, too, he thought, remembering all the days and nights they had spent together, the hours they had spent walking under the stars, holding hands. The times he had danced, just for her. All the nights he had gone home, hard and hurting, because she was a nice girl....

"Hey."

She stopped at the sound of his voice, but didn't turn around.

"I didn't mean to bark at you like that."

She turned slowly, not quite meeting his gaze.

He jerked his chin toward the corral. "He's wild, that one, fresh off the range. I just didn't want you to get hurt."

With a nod, she turned and walked down the trail.

He watched her until she was out of sight, admiring the sway of her hips, the way the sun cast blue highlights in her hair. Why had he felt the need to explain his reaction? Why did he care what she thought? Rationalizing, he told himself he couldn't afford to offend any of the guests, especially the rich spoiled ones who were accustomed to voicing their complaints when they didn't get their own way. He was here on sufferance, nothing more. But that wasn't the real reason, and he knew it.

He shook his head ruefully. He had sworn off white women. But he couldn't help admiring the view as she walked away.

Chapter Three

Cindy walked swiftly down the path toward the office, her cheeks burning with embarrassment. Of all the men in the world, Ethan Stormwalker was the last one she had ever expected to see again. Perversely, he was also the one she most wanted to see.

Ethan. He was still the most ruggedly handsome man she had ever known, from the top of his black-thatched head to the soles of his Lakota moccasins. She had hoped that if she ever saw him again, she wouldn't feel anything, proving that she was over him once and for all. For the first few weeks after they broke up, she had slept in one of his old T-shirts. She'd never washed it because it had smelled like Ethan, reminded her of Ethan. And then, when months had gone by and he still hadn't called, she had burned every letter, every picture, every gift he had ever given her except one. But the pain was still there, and now, after seeing him again, she knew it was never going to go away, that in spite of everything, she was still in love with him. If she were smart, she would leave here, now, this minute. And she was smart. But she was also hungry.

Her stomach growled loudly, reminding her that she hadn't eaten since breakfast early that morning. Checking the schedule posted outside the office, she saw that dinner was served from 5:30 to 7:00 p.m. If she hurried, she would just make it.

And why should she leave? she thought as she made her way to the lodge. She didn't want him to think that he had frightened her off. She had always wanted to visit a ranch. She was here. And she was going to stay, Ethan Storm-walker be damned!

The dining room was large and rectangular. An enormous fireplace took up most of one wall, a huge rack of antlers hanging over it. Two long trestle tables, with chairs enough to seat twenty-four people each, occupied the center of the room. A half dozen square tables lined the walls. A handful of people were still seated at one of the long tables, talking and laughing over apple pie and ice cream.

Feeling somewhat shy, Cindy took a seat at one of the smaller tables beside a window. A moment later the woman she had talked with in the office bustled into the room. She was tall and angular, her thick black hair just beginning to show streaks of gray.

"Miss Wagner," Dorothea Donovan said, smiling, "what are you doing sitting here all alone? Come on over and meet the Petersens."

"I'd rather not, if you don't mind," Cindy replied. She wasn't in the mood to make small talk, or explain why she was there by herself.

Dorothea frowned, and then smiled. "Whatever you wish. We're serving chicken tonight. I'll have Margie bring you a plate. What would you like to drink?"

"Milk?"

Dorothea patted her shoulder. "I need to go check some things at the office, but Margie's in the kitchen. She'll take good care of you. If there's anything you want, just ask for it.''

''Thank you.''

Dorothea beamed at her. She paused to speak to the Petersens for a few moments, then disappeared into the kitchen.

A short time later, a plump woman wearing a big blue-and-white checked apron brought Cindy a plate piled high with half a fried chicken, mashed potatoes, corn on the cob, a hot flaky biscuit and a tall glass of milk.

''I'm Margie,'' the woman said. ''If you want dessert, just holler.''

''Thank you.''

''Stormwalker is dancing tonight,'' Margie told her as she headed back to the kitchen. ''You don't want to miss that.''

Nodding, Cindy stared at the food on her plate, her mind filling with images of Ethan dancing at powwows. Of Ethan dancing just for her on warm summer nights, his copper-hued skin glowing, his hair silvered in the moonlight.

She pushed the memories away and concentrated on the food on her plate. She would never be able to eat it all, she thought as she took a bite of mashed potatoes. But she did. The chicken was tender and juicy, the potatoes and corn delicious. The biscuit melted in her mouth.

She was wondering what to do with her dishes when the family at the other table stood up. The woman paused beside Cindy.

''Just leave the dishes,'' she said with a friendly smile. ''You're new here, aren't you? I'm Flo Petersen, and this is my husband, Earl, and our kids, Linda, Nancy and Mary.''

''Cindy Wagner. Pleased to meet you.'' She smiled at the three girls, who couldn't have been much more than a year apart in age. They were pretty kids, with long blond ponytails and large, dark brown eyes. She thought the oldest was probably twelve or thirteen.

"We're on our way to watch the dancing," Flo said. "Would you like to come with us?"

Cindy hesitated, about to refuse, but the thought of watching Stormwalker dance was far too tempting to resist. "Yes, thanks."

Rising, she dropped her napkin on the table and followed the Petersens out of the dining room.

"There's some form of entertainment every night," Flo told her. "Movies, bingo, square dancing. And there are always games and such going on up in the game room at the lodge."

"Sounds like fun."

Outside, they fell in behind a number of people walking toward a large outdoor amphitheater. A fire burned in a shallow pit in the center, casting long shadows over the large tepee that stood to one side, and the faces of the three middle-aged men who sat around a large drum. The bleached buffalo skull beside the tepee seemed to leer at Cindy as she took a seat beside Flo.

"Stormwalker's dancing tonight," Flo said. "We saw him last week."

"He's dreamy," the oldest girl said, sighing.

"I'm afraid my Linda has quite a crush on him." Flo smiled fondly at her daughter. "When you see him, you'll know why."

"Shh," Linda said, leaning forward. "They're going to start."

A hush fell over the crowd as one of the drummers stood and introduced himself and the other two men. His words were lost on Cindy as Ethan stepped into view. He wore a loincloth and a pair of moccasins. His face and chest were streaked with black and white paint; a pair of eagle feathers were fastened in his hair on the left side. His muscles rippled as he stepped to the center of the floor; the bells he wore around his right ankle chimed softly as he moved. A wide copper band circled his left biceps.

He stood there a moment, his head bowed, his long black hair falling over his shoulders, hiding most of his face. He looked untamed and dangerous and utterly fascinating.

The beat of the drum started as no more than a whisper, like the sighing of a summer breeze. Slowly, he lifted his head, his dark eyes piercing the darkness, a predator assessing his hunting grounds. And then he began to move, his body weaving back and forth, the bells on his ankle a sharp counterpoint to the steady beat of the drum.

She watched him, mesmerized, remembering other dances, other nights. She had seen him perform this dance before, at a powwow. The dance portrayed a young warrior laying a trap for an eagle. He climbed a high mountain, dug a pit and covered it with brush, then crouched inside, waiting, and when the eagle came, he reached up through the brush and caught the bird's feet. She sensed his excitement, the danger, the thrill of the hunt.

As the beat of the drum increased, Ethan's steps grew faster and more intricate, but no less precise. There were times when his feet were no more than a blur. Perspiration sheened his body so that his skin seemed to glow in the firelight.

It was beautiful. Magical. Almost mystical.

The next dance was slower, softer, a courting dance. And after that came a friendship dance. The lead drummer invited everyone to participate. It was, he said, one of the oldest styles of Indian dancing. The steps were simple. Holding hands, everyone sidestepped to the left, starting with the left foot and moving in a circular manner.

Cindy grinned as she noticed that Linda managed to grab one of Ethan's hands as they made a large circle around the firepit.

Cindy kept her gaze on her feet, afraid to meet Ethan's eyes, afraid of what he might see in hers.

When the dancing was over, she told Flo and her family good-night and walked back to her cabin. Knowing she couldn't put it off any longer, she kicked off her shoes, then sat down on the bed, took a deep breath, picked up the receiver and called home.

Her younger brother answered on the first ring. "Wagner residence."

"Hi, Lance, is Mom there?"

"Cindy Lou, hey, how ya doing? Nice wedding."

"Shut up, squirt. Let me talk to Mom."

There was a moment of silence, and then she heard her mother's voice.

"Cynthia? Where are you, sweetie? Are you all right? We've been so worried. You're not sick, or anything?"

"No, I'm fine, Mom. Really. I just couldn't go through with it." She heard her dad's voice in the background.

"Your father wants to know if you want him to come after you."

"Not right now."

"Have you talked to Paul?"

"No." Cindy fell back on the bed and stared up at the ceiling. "I wouldn't know what to say."

"Well, don't worry about it. I talked to his mother earlier this evening. Paul and his sister went to New York."

Cindy laughed. Trust Paul to forge ahead no matter what. It was always business first with him. He wouldn't let a little thing like a runaway bride interfere with that. "I hope they have a good time."

"Where are you?"

"Elk Valley Dude Ranch." Cindy paused a moment. "Mom? Don't tell Dad where I am, okay? If he asks, just tell him you don't know."

There was another moment of silence on the other end of

the line. "All right. Is there any reason why you feel that way?"

"I'm pretty sure Paul won't call asking for me, but just in case he does, I don't want him to know where I am. You understand?"

"Yes," Claire said, her tone neutral. "I understand perfectly."

"Oh, Mom, why didn't I listen to you?"

"Because you're stubborn and hardheaded, just like your father. How long do you plan to stay there?"

"I don't know. Is Dad very upset?"

She heard her mother take a deep breath. "Yes, very."

"I just couldn't do it, Mom."

"You did the right thing. Don't worry about it," Claire said, speaking much more softly than before. "I'm just glad you came to your senses before it was too late. And don't worry about your father. He'll come around, you'll see."

"I hope so."

She heard her father in the background, louder and more agitated this time, and then his voice rumbled over the phone. "Are you all right, Cindy Lou?"

"I'm fine, Dad. I'm sorry that—"

"I want this marriage," he interrupted gruffly. "Paul would be good for you, and you'd be good for him. He's got a good head on his shoulders and he'll—"

"Dad, I don't love Paul. I never did. I let the two of you talk me into something I never wanted."

"Cynthia…"

She closed her eyes and clenched her fist. "You can't change my mind, Dad. Not this time. I know what I'm doing."

She could feel the frost building on the other end of the line. There was a long pause, and then he said, "Very well. Your mother wants to say good-night."

There was a momentary silence, then her mom came on the phone again. "Keep in touch now, hear?"

"I will." She blinked back her tears. "I love you, Mom."

"I love you, too, sweetie. Good night."

"'Night."

Cindy took a quick shower and slipped into bed naked, thinking of all the beautiful nightgowns packed in her trousseau.

"Oh, well," she murmured. Turning on her side, she stared into the darkness, her mind filling with the sensual beat of a distant drum and the image of a tall, dark-skinned warrior with smoldering gray eyes.

Chapter Four

Cindy was at breakfast the next morning when Dorothea approached her. "If you're still looking for a ride to town, my nephew is getting ready to go," she said.

"Oh, yes, I am, thanks."

"He'll be leaving in a few minutes. You'll find him out front in the ranch pickup."

With a nod, Cindy left the table. She made a quick stop at her cabin to put on some lipstick, run a brush through her hair and grab her handbag.

The pickup, a big black truck, was waiting in front of the office. The picture of an elk's head was painted on the side, with the words *Elk Valley Dude Ranch* stenciled in neat white letters above its antlers.

Opening the passenger door, she climbed in. "Thanks for waiting for me," she said, "I..." Her voice trailed off as the driver turned to look at her. Her heart slammed against her chest. "Oh, it's you."

An emotion she didn't recognize flickered in his eyes and was quickly gone. "You got a problem with that, Miss Wagner?"

"No. No, of course not. I just didn't realize you were Dorothea's nephew."

"You ready to go, or have you changed your mind?"

She pulled the door closed with more force than was necessary and settled back in the seat, her arms crossed over her breasts. "How long does it take to get to town?"

"About an hour."

An hour. Alone with Ethan. She groaned inwardly. And another hour back. Before she could say she had changed her mind, he put the truck in gear and drove out of the yard.

They passed half a dozen guests returning from an early morning trail ride. Flo and her husband were among them. Cindy waved at the couple as they drove past.

It was a beautiful day, warm and clear outside. Frosty cold inside. Cindy kept her gaze focused on the view out the passenger-side window as the silence between them thickened. A heavy silence that made her decidedly uncomfortable.

She slid a glance at Ethan as they turned off the ranch road onto the highway. He wore a pair of snug jeans, a chambray shirt and moccasins. He had a strong profile, lean and rugged. There had always been something about him, she thought, a sort of power she had never sensed in anyone else. And now there was something more. It was as if he had erected a wall between them. He drove with his right hand on the wheel, his left arm resting on the window opening. A black hat lay on the seat between them.

As though feeling her gaze, he looked over at her. "What?"

"Nothing."

He grunted softly. "What are you doing here?"

"Excuse me?"

"At the ranch."

She hesitated a moment. "I'm on vacation."

"Alone?" He lifted one brow. "Boyfriend change his mind at the last minute?"

"I don't see as how that's any of your business, but no, he didn't. I…I came here on…on a whim."

"In a wedding dress?"

"If you must know, I changed my mind about getting married."

Amusement danced in his dark eyes. "Nothing like waiting till the last minute."

She felt a flush climb up her neck to her cheeks. Ethan had once accused her of being nothing but a spoiled rich girl. She looked out the window again. He was right, she thought. She was spoiled. And her parents were rich. But what difference did it make, anyway? There was no crime against being spoiled. And her father had worked hard to get where he was today. And why was she suddenly feeling so defensive?

Startled when Ethan touched her shoulder, she glanced over at him. "Look," he said. Slowing the truck, he pointed out the window on his side.

She leaned forward and looked past him to see a doe and two fawns standing in the dappled shade of a tree. "Oh, aren't they beautiful!"

"Yeah."

"I could never understand why anyone would want to kill something so beautiful just for a trophy."

"Well, lots of people do it."

"I know, although why anyone would want a deer's head on their wall is beyond me. I mean, what is there to brag about? It's not like killing a mountain lion with your bare hands, or anything."

"I always did like your way of thinking." He almost smiled at her; instead, he turned his attention back to the road. He should have got someone else to drive her into town, he thought. This trip had disaster written all over it.

"I need to pick up some supplies for the ranch," he said as he pulled into a parking place near the center of town. "How long do you think you'll be?"

"I'm not sure." She shrugged. "Two hours?"

He grimaced. "All right. I'll meet you back here at noon."

"Okay."

She got out of the truck, closed the door and stepped onto the sidewalk, conscious of his gaze on her back. She heard the truck pull away from the curb as she ducked into the first store she saw. When she was sure he was gone, she went back outside and started walking.

She had always loved shopping. It had been her way of celebrating the good times, or escaping the bad ones. Good grades, a fight with her mother, making the cheerleading team, a bad day on the tennis court, being picked as captain of the debate team, a bad haircut, or an argument with a boyfriend—whatever the occasion, Cindy had grabbed her dad's credit card and headed for the mall. Which probably explained why she had closets bulging with more clothes and shoes than any one woman could ever wear.

She bypassed one gift shop after another until she came to a large department store. Once inside, she quickly lost track of the time as she wandered through the aisles. She tried on whatever caught her eye, and in the end, bought three sundresses—one a bright yellow polka-dot, one a dark rose color with delicate white flowers embroidered along the hem, the third a dressier dark blue and lavender print with a matching jacket. She picked out a pair of white sandals, three pairs of jeans—blue, black and red—a half-dozen T-shirts in a variety of colors, four Western-style shirts, a pair of low-heeled cowboy boots, socks, underwear, a cotton nightgown, a terry-cloth robe and a pair of Ray Bans.

She was on her way to meet Ethan when she passed a shop filled with cowboy hats. She was standing in front of a mirror, her packages scattered at her feet, trying to decide between a white hat with a rolled brim or a tan hat with a flat brim when Ethan came up behind her.

He held up his arm and tapped his forefinger on his watch. "You're late," he said brusquely.

"Oh. Sorry. Which hat to do you like the best?"

"The tan one. White's impractical out here."

"All right. The tan one it is."

She picked up her packages and carried them, along with the hat, to the counter, aware of Ethan trailing at her heels like a dark cloud.

She paid for the hat and put it on, then followed him out to the boardwalk.

"So, how do I look?" she asked.

"Like a city girl in a cowboy hat," he drawled. He hesitated a moment, then said, "Do you want to grab some lunch before we head back to the ranch?"

"Do you?"

"I could eat. Let's put your packages in the truck."

She did as he suggested, noting that the back of the truck was loaded with boxes and bags. She shut and locked the door, then hurried after Ethan, who was walking slowly down the sidewalk.

At the end of the block, they crossed the street and entered the Cowboy Café. It was a small restaurant, not particularly crowded at this time of the day. There was a counter across from the door, booths along three of the walls.

Admiring the way his jeans fit his lean hips, she followed Ethan to a booth in the back near the window and slid in across from him.

Pushing his hat back on his head, he handed her a menu and took one for himself.

Cindy stared at the menu, wondering how she could possibly eat a bite with Ethan sitting across from her. All the memories she had tried so hard to banish from her mind came thundering back, as crystal clear as if they had happened yesterday.

She had been sixteen the first time she had seen him dance. It had been at a powwow, and she'd been there with her best friend. They had gone to the fairgrounds on a lark, thinking it would be fun to see some "real live Indians." Sherry had soon grown bored, but Cindy had been mesmerized by the low, throbbing beat of the drums, the dancing, the brightly colored costumes. The Indians had been friendly yet aloof. She had stayed long after Sherry's mother came to pick her up. During a break in the dancing, Cindy had wandered around the grounds, looking at dream catchers and rattles, gourds and pipes, bows and arrows. She had bought a small white horse with black spots adorned with turquoise feathers, a dream catcher, some fry bread. She had been leaving the fairgrounds when she'd bumped into Ethan. Literally. He had knocked her on her rump and she had sat in the dirt staring up at him, too tongue-tied to speak. He had been gorgeous. Tall, dark, handsome as sin, and a little mysterious, clad in his dance costume, his face streaked with black paint.

"Sorry," he'd said. He'd picked up her packages, then, offering her his hand, had helped her to her feet.

She'd muttered her thanks, then stared after him as he moved on down the fairway toward the dance area. He'd stood head and shoulders above most of the crowd, making it easy for her to follow him. She didn't know if he was going to dance, but there was no way she was leaving, she decided. Not until she found out.

She'd located a seat on the end of a bench near the entrance to the dance area and sat down, wincing a little. A dozen or so dancers entered the arena, and he had been one of them. Her discomfort had been quickly forgotten when he began to dance, his steps light yet powerful. He wore a brightly colored costume and had long strands of what looked like ribbon hanging from his arms and waist. She had never seen anything so beautiful, so utterly mesmerizing. Why hadn't she brought her camera? She was wondering what the dance was about when she overheard a Native American woman explaining it to a white man and his wife.

"This is the grass dance," the woman said. "According to legend, there was once a young man who was lame. Even so, he longed to dance with the other warriors and so he went out onto the prairie to pray for guidance. He made his way up a small hill and when he reached the top, it came to him that he should create a dance of his own. As he was pondering this, he looked at the prairie spread out below him and noticed how the tall grasses swayed. That would be his dance. That is why men wear yarn or ribbons hanging from their arms and their waists while they dance, their steps making it flow like prairie grass rippling in the wind."

Cindy had applauded wildly when Ethan finished dancing. He had looked in her direction and smiled. It was the first time she had seen him smile, and it hit her like a thunderbolt. Lethal. Devastating. Utterly irresistible.

While waiting to see if he was going to dance again, she glanced at one of the pamphlets she had picked up from a booth. It was titled "Notes for Powwow Fans." Among other things, it advised watchers to rise when the eagle staff was brought into the arena during the grand entry, or if an eagle feather fell during the dancing. It mentioned that pointing was considered impolite, that the taking of pictures was allowed but flashes were not, and that one should ask permission before taking an individual's photograph. Costumes and ornaments were not to be touched, as some costumes cost many thousands of dollars, and bothering the performers or standing in front of those preparing to dance or sing would not be tolerated. A small note at the bottom added that the tribes did not dance for mindless amusement.

Dancing was a form of worship. The drum, with its round shape, represented the shape of the universe.

Cindy had stayed until the last dance and then headed for the parking lot, only then remembering that she didn't have a ride. With a sigh, she'd turned and headed back to the fairgrounds to look for a phone.

And bumped into Ethan a second time.

"It must be fate," he had said, grabbing her arm to steady her.

"It must be." He looked as sexy in black jeans and a T-shirt as he had in paint and feathers. "Do you know where I can find a phone?" she'd asked him.

"Over there, by the rest rooms."

"Thanks."

"I was about to go and get something to eat," he said. "I don't suppose you'd like to join me?"

He was inviting her out. She couldn't believe it! "I'd love to, but I need to call my dad to come and pick me up."

"I'm through here for the day. I can drive you home afterward."

Ordinarily, she would never have gotten in a car with a stranger, but, to her surprise, she had said, "That would be great. Thanks."

"Hey!" Ethan reached across the table and tapped her on the shoulder, bringing her back to the present. "You ready to order?"

"What? Oh, yes. I'd like a bacon, lettuce and tomato sandwich on sourdough bread, lightly toasted. And onion rings and a chocolate shake."

"And I'll have a cheeseburger, fries and coffee," Ethan told the waitress.

An uncomfortable silence fell between them when the waitress left to turn in their order. Cindy stared out the window, wondering why she hadn't jumped out of the truck the minute she saw him behind the wheel.

Sitting back in his seat, Ethan studied her profile. He had known from the beginning that getting mixed up with her would be a mistake. Young white girls were always trouble, but there had been something about her, about the way she looked at him, the way it made him feel, that he had been unable to resist. He had taken her out to dinner that first night, and everything she had told him only proved his first instinct had been right. She was going to be trouble. He had guessed her to be eighteen, and almost choked on his coffee when she told him she had just turned sixteen. The words *jail bait* had drifted through his mind, but the three years separating them didn't seem so great. The fact that she was rich had been another strike against her. Rich white girls were poison. He had taken her home, walked her to the door, told her good-night and left her there, never intending to see her again.

A week later, she had turned up at a powwow in a neighboring city. He had danced his heart out that afternoon, always aware that she was watching him and only him. It had been his best day on the circuit; he had won every competition he entered. He hadn't planned on talking to her, but when a dance break came, he found himself asking her if she wanted to go get something to eat when he was through, and next thing he knew, they were sitting in his truck tangled up in each other's arms. He had tried to remind himself that she was only a kid, but she hadn't kissed like a kid.

"Cheeseburger and fries?"

As the waitress brought their order, Ethan shook off his memories, glad for the distraction.

He picked up his coffee cup and took a drink. "So," he said, how long are you staying at the ranch?"

"I don't know." She poured ketchup on her plate. "Until I'm ready to go home."

He grunted softly, wondering what her folks thought of their runaway daughter.

"How long have you been working at the ranch?" she asked.

"About four years."

"I guess you must like it."

He shrugged. "It's a job." And better than jail.

She glanced surreptitiously at his left hand. "Are you married?"

"Hell, no."

She lifted one brow, puzzled by his curt reply. "I heard...that is, I thought...never mind."

"What did you hear?"

"That you were engaged."

"Yeah? Who'd you hear that from?"

"Sally Whitefeather."

He looked genuinely surprised. "I didn't know you and Sally kept in touch."

Cindy felt a wave of heat climb up her neck and into her cheeks. "We still talk now and then," she admitted reluctantly.

Ethan had introduced her to Sally at a powwow. Sally and Ethan had grown up together back on the rez. Sally had been Ethan's best friend. She had seemed the logical one to call when Cindy wanted to know what was going on in Ethan's life.

"So, are you?" she asked.

"Am I what?"

"Engaged," she said petulantly.

"No."

"Were you?"

"I was," he said, sounding as irritable as she did. The breakup had been Cindy's fault, though there was no way for her to know that. "What else did she tell you?"

Cindy took a bite of her sandwich, wishing they had never started this conversation. "She told me that you'd had a run-in with the law a while back."

Ethan swore under his breath. Cindy had been the cause of that, too, he thought.

"It's true, then?"

"So what?" He looked at her, his eyes as cold as his voice.

"Nothing." She pushed her plate away, her appetite gone.

"Are you ready to go?" he asked.

"Yes."

He finished his coffee, put down enough money to cover the check, and slid out of the booth.

Feeling miserable, Cindy followed him outside. She had wanted to ask him why he had never returned her call, but she hadn't been able to summon the nerve to bring up the past.

It was a long, quiet ride back to the ranch.

Chapter Five

Ethan dropped her off at her cabin when they returned to the ranch, then drove to the back of the lodge to unload the supplies. Of all the miserable luck, he thought, his had to be the worst. Why had she shown up here, of all places? She had been just a kid when he'd known her before, sixteen to his nineteen. But she was all grown up now.

When he finished unloading the truck, he drove to his place. He parked the truck beside the house, switched off the engine, grabbed his hat. Wolf met him as he stepped out, and Ethan spent a few moments scratching the dog's ears before going into the house to change his shirt and put on a pair of boots. He checked the clock, noting he had about twenty minutes before he was scheduled to take a group out on a trail ride.

Going into the kitchen, he grabbed a beer from the fridge, then went out onto the porch and sat on the steps. Wolf stretched out beside him.

Pushing his hat back on his head, Ethan took a long drink, then wiped his mouth with the back of his hand. "Why'd she have to come here?" he muttered.

Wolf growled in response.

"Damn." Draining the bottle, Ethan tossed it on the porch and stood up. His only hope was that she would soon get bored and go home where she belonged, back to her rich father and her big house and her fancy car.

He had driven by her house late one night soon after they first met. House? It was a mansion three stories high, surrounded by a wrought-iron fence with a uniformed guard at the gate. Ethan hadn't really paid much attention to the place the first time he'd seen it. But looking at it that night, he had known then and there that they had no future together. He couldn't begin to imagine what her parents would say if she brought him home to Sunday dinner. And when it happened a month later, it had been a worse disaster than even he had imagined. Jordan Wagner had looked at him as if his daughter had brought home a stray mutt and intended to keep it in the house; Claire Wagner had nervously touched her hair from time to time, as if checking to make sure he hadn't taken her scalp when she wasn't looking. At the dinner table, her father and mother had talked politely of the weather, inquired about his family, been openly shocked when he told them he earned a living dancing on the powwow circuit. When he'd departed, he was not invited back. Jordan Wagner had bid him a firm goodbye, his tone and expression clearly stating that Ethan would not be welcome in his home again.

With a shake of his head, Ethan went down the steps and followed the dirt path that led to the lodge. He couldn't think of anything worse than that meeting with Claire and Jordan Wagner, until he reached the stable and found Cindy waiting there with a half a dozen of the other guests. Rudy had already rounded up the horses. They were hitched to the corral fence, tails swishing lazily.

Cindy's eyes widened when she saw him, and he knew she wasn't there because she was eager to see him.

"Afternoon, ladies and gents." He nodded at the riders. This was an adults-only ride. The youngest couple looked to be in their early twenties, the oldest in their sixties. Cindy was the only one without a partner. "Any of you here already know how to ride? No? Well, that's okay, by the end of the day, you'll all be old hands. First thing we're gonna learn how to do is saddle up. Don't worry about these broomtails. They're all seasoned trail horses."

He spent the next few minutes pairing up horses and riders, saving his favorite mare for Cindy. But when he got to her, she shook her head. "That's okay, I've decided not to ride today."

He should have been relieved, but he wasn't. "Afraid to ride with me?"

She lifted her chin and squared her shoulders. "Of course not. I just figured you'd already had enough of me for one day."

"Honey," he said, his voice pitched low for her ears only, "I never had enough of you."

His words brought a warm flush to her whole body. Stunned, she could only stare at him.

"So, you ridin' this afternoon, or are you gonna run away again?"

"I never…" She bit down on her lower lip. "I'm riding, Mr. Stormwalker."

It was to his credit that he didn't look smug. Picking up the blanket draped over the saddle, he held it up.

"All right, cowboys." He nodded at Cindy. "And cowgirls. This is the way we saddle a horse. The blanket comes first…." He placed it on the back of the horse he had chosen for Cindy. "Be sure to smooth it out flat. A wrinkle in the blanket is uncomfortable for the horse and can cause sores."

He walked down the line, making sure everyone did it right, before returning to Cindy's mount. "All right, the saddle comes next. Make sure it's centered properly, then cinch it up tight. You, in the red hat, you'll need to give Freckles a little punch in the stomach, otherwise you can't cinch him up tight enough.''

Ethan cinched the saddle on Cindy's mare, going slow so the others could follow.

Afterward, he once again walked down the line, making sure all the cinches were fastened correctly.

"All right, ladies and gents, take up the reins, put your left foot in the stirrup and pull yourselves up into the saddle. Hang on to the saddle horn if you have to. That's right.''

When they were all mounted, Ethan swung up on his own horse, a rawboned Appaloosa with a roached mane and a wispy tail. The gelding wasn't much to look at, but he was the best trail horse on the ranch.

Ethan glanced over his shoulder to make sure everyone was ready. "If you want to go left, you pull on the left rein. If you want to go right, pull on the right one. Pulling back on both reins at the same time will bring your horse to a stop. Don't jerk on the reins. Any questions?''

"Will we see any wildlife?'' This from a middle-aged man with a camera dangling on a cord around his neck.

Ethan grinned. "That depends on the wildlife, but we usually see some deer this time of day.''

"Does my horse have a name?'' The question came from the female half of the twenty-something couple.

"His name is Dandy.''

The woman smiled. "Dandy. Thanks.''

"Anything else?'' Ethan asked. "All right. Everybody ready?''

There were nods and thumbs-up interspersed with calls of "okay'' and "let's ride.'' With a last glance at Cindy, Ethan clucked to Dakota and the big horse moved out. The other wrangler, Rudy Salazar, rode drag.

The trail for beginning riders was an easy one. It followed the stream for about a mile, then came to a fork. The left ranch led into the wilderness. The right one made a big loop that led back to the lodge. About a mile beyond the fork, the trail led up a gentle slope to a flat-topped ridge. Ethan usually stopped at the top so the riders could look out over the ranch and the countryside. From there, they went down the hill and rode through a meadow into a patch of woods. It was here that they generally saw deer. Squirrels and chipmunks were common sights along the trail. Now and then they saw a skunk, and on rare occasions a coyote. Eagles were often seen riding the air currents.

Ethan felt some of the tension drain out of him as they left the ranch behind. His ancestors had once roamed this land. It was only here, away from civilization, that he truly felt at home. He thought of the days he had spent behind bars. He would still be there if his aunt hadn't come to his rescue. She had put up the money to bail him out of jail, had given him a job and assured the judge it wouldn't happen again. The days he had spent behind bars had been the worst of his life.

He shook the memory from his mind.

At the top of the ridge, he traded places with Rudy.

Riding drag was a big mistake. Cindy was the last rider, and Ethan couldn't take his eyes off her. She rode easy in the saddle, swaying with the movement of her horse. She had a natural seat and it was a pleasure to watch her, even from the back. Her hair was longer than he remembered. How many times had he buried his face in the wealth of her hair, breathed in the floral scent of it, ran his fingers through the soft silky strands?

Damn! He wrenched his thoughts from Cindy. He had to stop thinking of her, had to stop tormenting himself with the past. It was over and done and there was no going back. He hadn't been good enough for her before and nothing had changed.

"Look!" someone called excitedly. "A deer!"

Rudy reined his horse to a halt and the other riders pulled up behind him. The man with the camera quickly snapped a picture. The doe's ears flicked back and forth, her body poised for flight.

The dude with the camera was about to take another photo when one of the riders sneezed. That quick, the doe was gone.

Cindy wished she had thought to buy a camera at the gift shop. The scenery was breathtaking—snow-capped mountains far off in the distance, jagged hills covered with spruce and pine, a winding stream, the verdant meadow. And over it all a sky so wide and so blue it almost hurt her eyes to look at it.

And Ethan. Was there ever a man who looked as good on a horse as he did? He rode tall and easy in the saddle, his hat pulled low, alert yet relaxed as he pointed out a young buck in the distance.

It pained her to be so close to him, to remember the way it had once been between them. Even now, she wasn't sure just what had gone wrong. They'd had a silly disagreement that had somehow escalated into a full-blown argument. She had said things she hadn't meant, things she regretted, though she couldn't remember now exactly what they had argued about except that it had had something to do with Ethan leaving town to take part in a powwow in the Midwest. She realized now how foolish she had been to fight with him over something so stupid. Dancing in powwows was how he had made his living. But she had been so young and so desperately in love, she couldn't bear the idea of being parted from him for more than a few hours, let alone a few months. He had accused her of being spoiled and selfish; she had accused him of being thoughtless and uncaring.

What she did remember was the heavy silence between them when Ethan drove her home that night. He had pulled up to the front gate and stopped the car. She had sat there, on the verge of tears, wishing he would apologize, that he would take her in his arms and kiss her.

Instead, he had said, "I'll call you."

And she had replied, "Don't bother." She had been sorry as soon as she said the words, but she had been too young and too proud to take them back.

Jumping out of the truck, she had punched in the code to open the gate, and ran up the long winding road to the house without looking back.

She had cried all the next day, and then she had put her pride in her pocket and called him. His mother had answered the phone. "Ethan left for Kansas City early this morning," Ellen Stormwalker had told her.

Cindy had hung up the phone, devastated by the knowledge that he had been so anxious to get away from her he had left town a day earlier than planned. She had hurried home from school every day, hoping that Ethan had called and left a message, but he never did. After a week of her moping around the house, her parents had decided she needed a change of scene. After graduation, they had taken her to Europe for the summer.

Cindy had called Sally Whitefeather as soon as she got back home, ostensibly to catch up on Sally's life. In reality, she had wanted to know if her friend had heard from Ethan. When Sally had told her Ethan was engaged, Cindy felt sick to her stomach. Determined to put him out of her mind, she had gone away to college. She had met Paul during her junior year; Paul had been a senior. He had come home with her over Christmas vacation to meet her parents. Paul and her father had hit it off immediately. Jordan had taken Paul golfing, and introduced him to the men at his club. Looking back, Cindy realized Paul had spent more time with her father than he had with her. Funny, it hadn't bothered her at the time. Naturally, her father had been thrilled when she and Paul announced their engagement. Paul was everything Ethan wasn't.

And that, she thought, was the very reason why she had run away.

Looking up, she saw an eagle floating gracefully on the air currents. They were beautiful birds. Seeing it reminded her of the eagle feather Ethan had given her. He had told her that the Lakota believed that eagles carried messages to the Great Spirit. The feather was the only thing he had given her that she hadn't thrown away.

"Ethan…"

"You want something?"

Startled, she looked up, unaware she had spoken his name aloud. She stared at him blankly for a moment, then said the first thing that came into her mind. "Why were you in jail?"

His eyes went flat and hard. "What difference does it make?"

"None. I just wondered."

"You always were a nosy broad."

"I'm not a 'broad.'"

"Maybe not, but you're still nosy," he retorted, and urged his horse into a lope.

She stared after him, grieving for what they had lost, wishing she could summon the nerve to ask him why he had never called.

He was dancing again that night. Flo invited Cindy to go with her and her girls, but she declined. Being near Ethan, seeing him, talking to him, stirred too many memories— happy memories that were painful to recall because they reminded her of how much she had missed him. In college, she had spent far too many nights thinking of him, wondering who he was dating, if he was married. She had been swamped with jealousy for a woman she didn't know, one who might not even exist. But in her mind's eye, Cindy had pictured another woman watching him dance, going to the movies with him, taking walks, going for drives in the country. And always, in the back of her mind, was the knowledge that it could have been her if she hadn't been so foolish, so immature.

Standing outside her cottage, looking up at the stars, she heard the drum begin to beat. Closing her eyes, she imagined she could feel the beat of the drum rising up from the ground, surrounding her, enveloping her. Ethan had told her the drum was the heartbeat of the people.

With a sigh, she looked up at the stars again. *Star light, star bright, first star I see tonight, I wish I may, I wish I might, have the wish I wish tonight.* Sooner or later she would have to go home and face her family and friends. She wasn't sure which was worse, staying here and being tormented by Ethan's nearness, or going back home and trying to explain why she had left Paul at the altar.

The sound of applause rose on the air, and suddenly she was running across the yard toward the amphitheater. Breathless, she stopped at the entrance and then found a seat near the back, where Ethan wouldn't be able to see her.

As she watched him, the crowd seemed to fade into the distance, and all Cindy was aware of was Stormwalker. He was wearing a roach headdress, a beaded choker, a vest made of bones, a breechclout dyed red, a red-and-white bustle and moccasins. He wore bells around his ankles, a slash of red paint across one cheek.

A thrill of excitement shot through her. He looked wild, primitive, dangerous, just the way she had always imagined Indians looked in the past. She had always loved Native American legends and the history of the Old West; it had been her major field of study in college.

Her heart seemed to beat in time with the drum as she watched him dance. He was halfway through the next dance when he paused, his gaze searching the crowd. She knew the moment he saw her, felt the electricity flow between them, vital and alive.

And when he resumed dancing, his steps were faster, more sensuous, and she knew he was dancing just for her, as he had so often in the past.

As soon as he finished the last dance, she hurried out of the amphitheater and back to her cottage. Once inside, she paced from room to room, and then, too agitated to sleep, she went outside. For a moment she stood there, undecided, and then she turned and followed the path along the river, heading the opposite direction from his bungalow.

It was a beautiful clear night. A gentle wind whispered through the cottonwood trees. Crickets chirped. She heard a horse whinny in the distance, the faint sounds of a country song from inside the lodge. Passing by, she looked in the window. Several couples were line dancing. With a sigh, Cindy moved on. She really was out of place here, she thought. It was all families or couples, except for her.

She walked until the lights from the lodge were behind her, and then she walked down to the riverbank and sat down on a rock. Moonlight danced and shimmered on the water. A fish jumped.

She stared into the slow moving river, wishing she could turn back time, wishing she could recall the words she had spoken so rashly. But it was too late.

Chapter Six

Cindy rose early after a restless night. Dressing quickly in a pair of jeans and a navy blue T-shirt, she pulled on her boots, put on her hat and went up to the lodge. The dining room wasn't open yet, but she heard noise coming from the kitchen, and when she peeked inside, she saw the cook getting ready to fix breakfast. He was a tall man with close-cropped, dark brown hair and brown eyes. He wore a white apron over a white T-shirt and jeans. She thought he looked more like one of the wranglers than a cook.

"Hi," Cindy called. "I'd like to go for a walk. Would it be possible for me to get a cup of coffee and a sweet roll to eat on the way?"

Looking up, the cook wiped his hands on his apron. "Sure thing."

A few minutes later, Cindy left the lodge. She turned down the path that led to the trail alongside the river. The coffee was rich and wonderful, the roll freshly made. Dropping the paper cup into a trash can, she was about to continue on down the trail when she heard a horse whinny. Veering off the trail, she walked up to the barn.

A teenage boy wearing an Elk Valley Ranch T-shirt was saddling a string of horses.

"Hi," Cindy said.

"Mornin'," he replied. "You're up early."

"Would it be all right if I took one of the horses out for a little while?"

"I can't go with you until Rudy or Ethan gets here."

"That's all right. I just want to ride around the lodge. I don't think I'll get lost."

He frowned. "I don't know...."

She smiled at him. "I won't go far."

"All right. Here, take Jilly. She doesn't look like much, but she's easygoing and has a nice gait."

"Thank you."

The wrangler was right. Jilly didn't look like much. The mare had a mousy-brown coat and a scraggly mane and tail, but she had wide intelligent eyes, a smooth rocking-chair gait and a soft mouth.

Yesterday was the first time in years since Cindy had been on a horse. Like many young preteen girls, she had been horse happy, and because her parents had rarely denied her anything, they had given her riding lessons.

She rode the mare at a walk and a trot around the outskirts of the ranch yard, but quickly grew bored with that. She was about to go back to the stable when she saw the marker for the trail they had ridden the day before. It had been an easy ride, as she recalled, the trail wide and well-defined. She hesitated only a moment, then urged Jilly forward. Surely there could be no harm in riding a short distance from the ranch. The trail was for beginners, after all.

It was quiet this time of the morning, peaceful, with nothing but birdsong and the muffled clop-clop of the mare's hooves to break the stillness. Cindy thought briefly of home, but thinking about all that waited for her there was just too depressing, so she put it out of her mind, determined to enjoy her ride. The sky was blue, the air was crisp and clear, and, like Scarlett, she would worry about her troubles tomorrow.

She smiled at the squirrels and chipmunks she saw, urging Jilly into a lope when she saw a skunk nosing around near the edge of the trail.

When she came to the fork in the road, she paused. Yesterday, they had gone to the right. "What do you say, Jilly?" she remarked, reining the horse to the left. "Shall we go see something new?"

Riding on, she lost track of the time, her mind shying away from everything but the beauty of the world around her and the rolling gait of the mare. The trail twisted back and forth, cutting through the woods, climbing small hills, crossing back and forth across the river, then straightening out and rising sharply.

Gradually, Ethan made his way into her thoughts. Cindy wished she had asked Sally for more information about what he had been doing the past few years, but when Sally had told her Ethan was engaged, the news had come as such a shock that Cindy had mumbled some hasty excuse and hung up the phone. Belatedly, it occurred to her that he might be divorced. The fact that he wasn't married now didn't mean he had never married at all. Just thinking of it made her burn with jealousy. But surely if he'd been married before, he would have mentioned it. Then again, maybe not. He didn't seem inclined to talk about his past. She wondered again why he had been in jail.

With some surprise, Cindy noticed it was getting dark. She couldn't have been gone *that* long, she thought. Looking up, she saw dark gray thunderheads rolling across the sky, heard the distant sound of thunder. Lightning scored the clouds, followed by a crash of thunder, louder this time.

She was about to turn Jilly back toward the ranch when she realized that, while she had been daydreaming about

Ethan, she had somehow left the trail. Reining the mare to a halt, she glanced around, looking for a familiar landmark, only to realize that she was hopelessly lost.

The clouds swirled overhead, growing darker by the moment, and then the sky unleashed a torrent of rain. In less than a minute, she was soaked to the skin.

A blinding flash of lightning split the skies. There was the smell of ozone, then a loud crack as a tree off to her right burst into flame. Jilly reared and came down running. Cindy pulled back on the reins, but the mare had the bit in her teeth and took off in a dead run, streaking across a stretch of open prairie. Wind and rain stung Cindy's eyes and whipped her hair into her face. Her hat went flying, blown away by a fierce gust.

Her legs clamped to the mare's sides, Cindy clutched the saddle horn in a death grip, praying that the horse wouldn't slip on the wet grass or step in a hole.

She pulled on the reins again, but to no avail. The horse had been royally spooked and wasn't about to stop. Clinging to the pommel as though it was a lifeline, Cindy could only hang on and pray that the mare knew her way home, that they would get there in one piece.

The prairie gave way to a wooded slope. As the mare lost her footing, Cindy screamed and toppled out of the saddle sideways, crying out as she hit her head against a fallen branch. The mare slid down the muddy slope on her haunches, gained her feet and took off running again.

Cindy lay there for a moment, too stunned to move, her head throbbing. Gradually, she became aware of a sharp pain in her right ankle. Feeling sick to her stomach, she sat up. When she touched the side of her head, her fingers came away covered with blood.

Ethan slept late and woke in a foul mood. He dressed in a pair of jeans and a T-shirt, pulled on his moccasins, settled his hat on his head. Going into his kitchen, he looked around, then decided to go up to the lodge for a cup of George's coffee.

He nodded at a handful of guests hurrying up to the lodge. There was a storm brewing. He could smell the rain in the air. The weather suited his mood perfectly, he thought. In the dining room, he found a table in the back near a window and sat down.

Millie Brown sashayed up to his table. "We've got waffles or bacon and eggs for breakfast." She poured him a cup of coffee. She was a pretty girl, with curly red hair, brown eyes and a ready smile. She had been working at the ranch about eight months, and made no secret of the fact that she wanted to go out with him. But so far he'd shied away from asking her out. Once burned, twice shy.

After ordering, Ethan picked up his coffee cup and took a sip. Against his will, he found himself thinking of Cindy, wondering where she was, what she was doing. He glanced around the room, but there was no sign of her. Had she had breakfast yet? Glancing outside, he saw that the sky had turned dark. Lightning flashed in the distance. He'd have to cancel the afternoon trail ride.

"You're late," Dorothea said, coming up behind him.

"Yeah." He jerked his chin at the chair across from his. "Join me?"

She smiled as she sat down. "Something troubling you, Nephew?"

He glowered at her. "No, why?" It was raining now, the first light drops spattering against the window.

Dorothea shook her head. She was a tall, angular woman with brown hair and blue eyes. She had never been pretty, yet she had aged well. For all her years, there was no gray in her hair, and there was still a spring in her step. She'd been running the ranch by herself since her husband, Ethan's uncle, had died two years before.

"Don't lie to me, young man. I've known you your whole life. Now, what's stuck in your craw?" She studied him through narrowed eyes when he didn't answer. "Can only be one of two things," she mused. "Money or a woman. I'm guessing it's the latter."

Ethan swore softly. His aunt saw too much by half.

Millie set a plate in front of Ethan, then looked over at Dorothea. "Can I bring you anything, Mrs. Donovan?"

"No, thanks, Millie." Dorothea waited until the waitress left the table, then leaned forward. "It's time you put the past behind you, Nephew. You need to go out once in a while. Why don't you ask Millie out? It's easy to see the girl's crazy about you."

"Dorothea…"

"You're my kin," she interjected. "That gives me the right to interfere. I don't like seeing you keep to yourself so much. If you're not interested in Millie, why don't you cozy up to that pretty Miss Wagner?"

At the mention of Cindy's name, Ethan almost choked on his coffee.

"I know she's only here for a short time," Dorothea added, "but what could it hurt to take her out to dinner and a movie?"

"Speaking of Miss Wagner, have you seen her this morning?"

"Why, no, I haven't," Dorothea said, beaming at him. "She probably slept late. I'll bet she'd love to take in a movie. You ask her now, hear?"

Blowing out a sigh of exasperation, Ethan pushed away from the table. If there was one thing he didn't need, it was a matchmaker. "I'll see you later."

The rain was coming down harder now. Ethan hunched his shoulders and sprinted across the yard toward the cabins, wondering what possible excuse he could give Cindy for showing up at her bungalow. She had made it perfectly clear she wouldn't welcome his company, and he for damn sure didn't want to get tangled up with her again. So what was he doing standing here in the rain, knocking on her door?

He waited a moment, then knocked again, louder. Surely she wasn't still in bed at this hour? It was after eleven.

Frowning, he put his hand on the knob and gave it a turn. The door opened and he poked his head through the doorway. "Cindy?"

Even as he called her name, he knew the cabin was empty. He had always been able to sense when she was around, and she wasn't here.

Closing the door, he walked over to the game room. Due to the rain, the place was crowded. Kids were playing video and board games; a few were watching cartoons.

The adults were reading, or playing cards, or just chatting. There was no sign of Cindy.

He checked the laundry room, stopped by her cabin again and then headed for the barn.

Rudy looked up from the horse he was grooming. "Hey, Ethan, don't suppose we'll be doing any riding today."

"No. Have you seen Miss Wagner?"

"Not since yesterday. Hey, Alex, have you seen Miss Wagner?"

The teenage boy Dorothea had hired for the summer poked his head out of the tack room in the back of the barn. "I don't know her name, but some lady came in this morning and took one of the horses out."

"What did she look like?"

Alex smiled. "She was real pretty, with long black hair and—"

"You let her go out alone?" Ethan asked sharply.

"Well, she said she was just gonna ride around the yard, so I…"

Ethan glanced at his watch. "How long ago did she leave?"

Alex shrugged. "A couple hours, I guess. Why?"

Ethan swore under his breath. "What horse did she take?"

"I put her up on Jilly."

Ethan glanced at Jilly's stall. It was empty.

"I'm sorry, Mr. Stormwalker."

"You think she's in trouble?" Rudy asked.

"I don't know...." Ethan's voice trailed off as he heard the muffled sound of hoofbeats. Glancing past Rudy, he swore under his breath as Jilly trotted into the barn.

Ethan grabbed the mare's reins. "Easy, girl." His gaze moved quickly over her, checking for signs of injury.

"She doesn't look hurt," Rudy said.

"No. Rudy, go up to the lodge and tell Millie to pack me some grub. Enough for a day or two. Alex, you get me a couple of blankets and a first aid kit. And don't say anything to Dorothea. No sense worrying her until we know there's something to worry about."

Alex hurried out of the barn.

"You think the woman's hurt?" Rudy asked.

"I don't know." Ethan thrust the mare's reins into Rudy's hand. "I'm going over to my place to grab a jacket and some gloves. If you get back here before I do, throw the grub in my saddlebags, will ya? Oh, and look after the buckskin till I get back."

"Sure."

Ethan saddled Dakota, then rode over to his place. Inside, he donned a heavy sheepskin jacket, changed his moccasins for boots, grabbed a pair of fur-lined gloves, a flashlight, matches, a change of clothes and his rifle. He paused a moment, then, certain he had everything he needed, went outside. He slid the rifle into the saddle boot, then swung onto Dakota's back. Wolf whined low in his throat.

"Come on, boy," Ethan said.

Rudy and Alex were waiting for him when he got back

to the barn. Rudy had packed his saddlebags. Dismounting, Ethan checked the contents, then secured them behind the cantle.

Swinging into the saddle, he pulled on his gloves and rode out of the barn.

He made one more stop before leaving the ranch. Going to Cindy's cabin, he found one of her T-shirts and let Wolf sniff it.

"Find her for me," he said. Giving in to temptation, he buried his face in the soft cotton. "Please let her be all right," he murmured, and tucking the shirt inside his jacket, he left the cabin.

Outside, he swung into the saddle and took up the reins. Dakota shook his head against the rising wind, then broke into an easy trot. Wolf loped alongside.

Ethan swore under his breath as lightning ripped the skies. He hoped to hell he would find Cindy on the trail, walking back to the ranch, but that hope gradually died as more and more miles went by. Something was wrong. He knew it. Felt it deep in his gut. What the devil had possessed her to take off on her own? He would have bet money she had more sense than to go riding so far from the ranch with a storm brewing. With every passing mile, his sense of dread increased. Damn, anything could happen to a woman riding out here alone. She could have been thrown, could have fallen over a cliff and broke her neck. Could have been bit by a snake, mauled by a bear....

He felt a sudden coldness in the pit of his stomach when he found her hat lying on the prairie, flattened by the rain. It was an omen, he thought. A bad one.

Cindy sank down on a log, her hands lightly massaging her ankle. She was wet clear through and chilled to the bone. She had tried walking for a little while, but she hadn't made much progress, and the prospect of slipping in the mud and injuring her ankle even more was all too real. Besides, she had no way of knowing if she was even going in the right direction. She seemed to remember reading somewhere that if you got lost in the woods, you should just sit down and wait for someone to find you. And right now, with her head pounding and her ankle throbbing like Lakota war drums, that seemed like good advice.

If only it would stop raining. She hunched over, shivering uncontrollably while the storm raged all around her. She had never been so cold and miserable in her whole life. Or so scared. What if no one came looking for her? She dismissed the thought as soon as it was born. Of course someone would come looking for her…. Ethan would come. She knew it as surely as she knew she was hopelessly lost.

She wondered how long she had been gone and how long it would take before someone missed her. An hour? Two? Three? She looked up at the sky. Years ago, Ethan had taught her to tell time by the sun, but that was impossible now. What time was it? What if no one came? The thought of spending the night in the open, in the dark, sent a chill down her spine. For all that this was the twenty-first century, there were still wild animals in this part of the country. Wolves. Coyotes. Bears. Snakes.

She shook off her fanciful thoughts. Jilly would go back to the ranch and someone would come looking for her.

Her head jerked up as she heard what sounded like a wolf howling. And then she had the strangest feeling that Ethan was nearby. Eyes narrowed, she peered into the pouring rain and suddenly he was there, riding toward her on horseback, his big dog beside him.

"Cindy!" He was on the ground and running toward her before his horse had stopped moving.

She had never been so happy to see anyone in her whole life.

He knelt in front of her. "Are you all right?"

She nodded, tears of relief pouring down her cheeks.

"Come on." He took her by the arm and lifted her to her feet. "Let's get out of here."

She cried out as she put weight on her right foot.

"What is it?" he asked, his brow lined with concern.

"My ankle. I guess I sprained it when Jilly threw me."

"You were thrown?" His gaze moved over her. "Do you hurt anywhere else?"

"My head. Here."

His fingers gently probed the egg-size lump on the back of her skull, and then he swung her into his arms, lifted her onto the back of his horse and climbed up behind her.

Taking up the reins, he clucked to the gelding.

Cindy leaned back against Ethan, her head resting on his shoulder. He had come for her and there was nothing more to fear. Even the pain in her head seemed less severe, now that he was here, her knight in shining armor.

She was half-asleep when he reined the horse to a halt. Opening her eyes, she looked around. "Where are we?"

He slid over Dakota's rump. Removing the saddlebags from behind the cantle, along with two blankets rolled in plastic, he slung them over his shoulder, then came around and lifted her into his arms. "We're going to stay here until the storm passes."

"Here? Here where?" she asked, and then she saw it, a small square building neatly camouflaged by towering trees and brush.

He climbed the two steps to the covered porch. The door creaked loudly when he opened it. "Wolf, stay."

The dog whined softly, then dropped down on its belly.

Carrying Cindy inside, Ethan closed the door.

"Will your dog be all right out there?" she asked.

"He's used to it."

"What is this place?"

"It belongs to the ranch. We use it during hunting season."

"Oh."

Ethan lowered her to the cot in the corner and in no time at all had a cheery fire going in the hearth.

"Let's get you out of those wet clothes," he said.

As cold and wet as she was, she had no desire to undress in front of him.

"Here." He reached into his jacket and withdrew her T-shirt, then pulled a warm flannel shirt out of his saddlebags, along with a pair of thick wool socks. "You can wear these." He removed the plastic from the blankets. "And wrap up in one of these."

She stared up at him, unmoving.

"Don't worry, you can change while I look after my horse." And so saying, he went outside.

Dakota stood with his head down, his back to the wind. Taking up the reins, Ethan led the gelding to the lean-to in the back. Wolf trailed at his heels. He tied the gelding to a post with a rope he found hanging on a nail, then stripped the rigging from the horse and set it aside. Using a piece of old toweling, he dried the gelding as best he could, then took up the saddle, bridle and blanket and carried them into the shack.

Silent as a shadow, Wolf followed his master back to the cabin, then stretched out beside the door.

Taking a deep breath, Ethan entered the shack. Cindy had changed clothes. She was sitting on the bed with her back against the wall, the blanket draped around her shoulders. She looked mighty appealing sitting there, with her bare legs peeking from under the hem of his shirt. He noticed she had spread her wet clothes over the back of a chair in front of the fire.

Ethan removed his hat and hung it on a peg beside the

door, then shrugged out of his jacket and draped it over one of the other chairs.

She was watching him, waiting, he thought, to see if he was going to take off his T-shirt and jeans. He pulled off his boots and socks and T-shirt, but kept his pants on.

Glancing at her from the corner of his eye, he almost laughed aloud at the look of relief on her face.

Opening one of the saddlebags, he pulled out a thermos of hot coffee, poured a cup and handed it to her. After one sip, she looked as if she had died and gone to heaven.

"I'd better check your ankle," he said.

"Don't tell me you're a doctor, too?"

"Heap big medicine man," he replied, grinning faintly.

She bit down on her lower lip as he examined her foot and ankle.

"I'm no expert, but I don't think it's broken," he remarked. "Still, you've got a bad sprain there."

She winced when he ran his fingers over the bump on her head.

He grunted softly. "You might have a concussion."

"It hurts like the devil."

"I'm not surprised." Reaching into his saddlebag again, he withdrew the first aid kit. Rummaging inside, he found a bottle of aspirin. He opened the bottle and shook two tablets into her hand. Reaching into his saddlebag yet again, he pulled out a bottle of water and offered it to her.

"Thanks."

After she swallowed the aspirin, he took an elastic bandage from the kit and wrapped it around her ankle. "Are you hungry?"

When she nodded, he pulled a couple of sandwiches out of his saddlebags. "We've got ham and cheese or roast beef," he said, holding them up.

"Ham, please."

He handed her one of the sandwiches, then went to stand

in front of the fireplace in hopes of drying out his jeans. They ate in silence, passing the coffee cup back and forth between them.

Cindy glanced around. There wasn't much to see. Aside from the bed, there was the chair Ethan sat in, a small square table that looked like it had come from the bargain basement at the Goodwill, the two chairs holding their clothes, a stove, a cupboard and a dusty elk head over the fireplace.

By the time she finished eating, she could scarcely keep her eyes open.

"I don't think you should go to sleep," Ethan said, frowning.

"I have to. I'm so tired." She stretched out on the cot. "Just for a little while…"

A moment later, she was asleep.

Ethan covered her with the other blanket, then pulled the chair closer to the cot and sat down. Maybe she *was* just tired, he thought, but maybe that bump on her head was worse than he thought.

He was more worried about her than he wanted to admit. Going to the window, he stared out into the gathering darkness. For a moment, he debated the wisdom of trying to get back to the ranch, but then dismissed the idea. It was still raining. The trail would be treacherous now, especially at the first river crossing, which was most likely flooded.

Muttering an oath, he turned away from the window. They were better off here, at least for the time being. The shack was warm and dry, and they had enough food for a couple days, if necessary.

He sat down in the chair again, his gaze moving over Cindy's face. Damn, but she was even more beautiful than he remembered. Leaning forward, he shook her shoulder. "Cindy? Wake up."

Her eyelids fluttered open. "What's wrong?"

"Do you know your name?"

"What?"

"Your name, what is it?"

She frowned at him, then lifted a hand to her head. "Are you crazy?"

"Dammit…"

"My name is Cindy, I live in Montana and you're being ridiculous."

He grunted softly and then grinned at her. "I read somewhere that if you think someone has a concussion, you should wake them every hour."

"Every hour?" she said, groaning. "You've got to be kidding."

Leaning forward, he placed his hand on her brow.

She knew he was only checking to see if she had a fever, but awareness flowed through her, sparked by his nearness, by the touch of his hand.

"Why'd you run out on him?"

"Who? Oh, Paul." She blew out a sigh. "He was too rich. Too controlling. Too much like my dad." *And he wasn't you.*

"I didn't know you could be too rich," Ethan muttered. "But I know all about being too poor." He looked at her speculatively. "So, did you really leave him at the altar?"

"Yes. I don't know why I let it go so far. There's no excuse, really…." Sitting up, she propped the pillow behind her back. "I guess it was just easier to let him take over."

"Did you finish college?"

"Yes," she replied, and then lifted one brow. "How did you know I went?"

His gaze slid away from hers. "Sally must have mentioned it."

"You talked to her about me?" she asked, pleased.

He shrugged. "Now and then."

"We talked about you, too."

"Is that right?"

Cindy nodded. "Sally must have spent a lot of time on the phone."

"Yeah." Sally had never told him that Cindy asked about him. Why hadn't she ever mentioned it? And what would he have done if he knew?

"We had some good times, didn't we?"

"Yeah." His gaze met hers. This was no time to be going down memory lane, he thought ruefully. Not here, not now, when they were alone and vulnerable. But he couldn't help it. "Do you remember the night Sally snuck out of her house and then couldn't get back in because she forgot her key?"

"Yes." Cindy grinned. "And you got the bright idea that you could climb up the trellis outside her bedroom and swing over to the window."

"I made it, didn't I?"

"You almost broke the trellis and your neck, too."

"Well, I got her in the house, didn't I? And her parents never found out."

"My hero." Cindy's tone was light, but there was a wealth of emotion in her eyes.

Was she remembering the first time she had called him that? They had been out walking and found a baby bird at the base of a tree, chirping piteously for its mother. Cindy had called him her hero when he returned the tiny creature to its nest.

Awareness hummed between them again. It was a good thing she was hurt, he thought, or he would be sorely tempted to crawl into that bed beside her. The attraction between them had always been powerful, undeniable. But there had been more to their relationship than that. Cindy had always looked for the best in him, always made him see the best in himself.

He cleared his throat. "So, how are you feeling? Head still hurt?"

"A little." She yawned behind her hand.

"Go back to sleep."

"I think I will." She slid back under the covers. "You should get some sleep, too."

"Don't worry about me."

Their gazes met and held for a long moment. She wanted to say she'd done nothing but worry about him, think of him, dream of him for the last five years, but she wasn't sure that would be wise, or that he would want to hear it.

She closed her eyes, as much to avoid his gaze as anything else, but she could still feel him watching her, like a cat at a mouse hole.

Sleep was a long time coming and even then she couldn't escape him. Her dreams were filled with images of a barechested Lakota warrior swooping down on her and carrying her away on a big buckskin stallion.

Chapter Seven

Ethan kept watch over her all through the night, waking her every hour or so, checking her pupils. As annoying as it was to have her sleep disturbed so often, it also made her feel cherished. He had checked her one more time an hour ago. She had assured him she felt fine, and had insisted he get some sleep. She looked at him now, stretched out on the cot. He was so tall, so broad, he barely fit on the narrow mattress.

Just looking at him did funny things to her heart. Ethan had given her her first kiss, had been her first serious crush. But for his innate sense of honor and decency, she would have lost her virginity years ago. She blushed, remembering how she had begged him to make love to her, and how humiliating it had been when he refused, telling her she was too young to make such a life-altering decision. She had been stung by his words. Too young? she had thought angrily. She had been sixteen and certain she was all grown up. Only now did she realize how right he had been, and how very young sixteen really was.

With Ethan, she had never been afraid of anything, not even her father. When her dad had objected to her seeing Ethan, she had defied him for the first time in her life. Her parents had been wise enough to know that grounding her would only make her more defiant, and so they had agreed to let her date Ethan providing he picked her up at the front door and had her home at a decent hour.

In time, her mother had grown somewhat fond of Ethan, and though Cindy had doubted she would ever fully approve of her daughter dating an Indian dancer, Claire had done her best to make Ethan feel at home. It had been Claire who had tried to comfort Cindy when she broke up with Ethan, assuring her that she was too young to be serious about any man, and that, when the time was right, she would find someone else.

Cindy had thought Paul was that someone, right up until she stood beside him at the altar.

With a sigh, she collected her clothes from in front of the fireplace. Turning her back to the bed, she slipped out of Ethan's shirt and into her own jeans and T-shirt. Sitting down on the chair once again, she pulled on her socks and boots, then ran a hand through her hair. She needed a hairbrush. And a toothbrush, she thought, grimacing.

As quietly as possible, she crossed the floor and poured herself a cup of coffee from the thermos. Thanks to Ethan's tender care, the swelling in her ankle had gone down considerably and hardly hurt at all. She rummaged around in his saddlebags, looking for something to eat. She pulled out a sweet roll and a big red apple, then sat down again, her gaze resting on Ethan's face. She sat there for a long time, looking from Ethan to the window and back again.

It was still raining, though not as hard as the night before.

She wondered if anyone was out looking for them. Probably not, she decided. Anyone who knew Ethan knew he could take care of himself. He had told her that he had been raised on the reservation, and that his grandfather had taught him how to hunt and track and survive off the land.

It was morning when he woke to find her sitting there, watching him. He lifted one brow, his expression amused.

Cindy shrugged. "There's nothing else to look at."

Sitting up, he ran his hand through his hair. He glanced at the thermos on the table. "Any coffee left?"

"A little."

When she started to get up, he motioned for her to stay where she was. "I'll get it. I don't want you walking around on that ankle any more than you have to."

She smiled at him, obviously pleased by his concern.

He uncorked the thermos and poured the last of the coffee into the cup. Moving to the window, he looked outside. It was still raining, but the clouds were drifting. With any luck, the storm would blow itself out by nightfall and they could head back to the ranch tomorrow morning.

He could see Cindy's reflection in the glass. Hard to believe that, after all this time, after all that had passed between them, he still wanted her. Shoot, maybe it was just a bad case of lust. Maybe that was all it had ever been. It still galled him that she had refused his phone calls, that she hadn't answered his letters. He couldn't believe she'd been so angry with him that she had cut him out of her life. When he got back home from the powwow, he had gone to see her first thing, only to learn from the maid that the Wagners had gone to Europe for an extended holiday.

Setting the cup on the window ledge, he clenched his hands into fists. Maybe it wasn't so hard to understand. Hell, she had only been seventeen. Ethan had known from the start that getting involved with her would be a mistake, but he had been captivated by her from the beginning, charmed by her innocence, her unbridled admiration. She had made him feel as if anything was possible, made him believe in happily ever after. And then, the first time he'd had to leave her, she had thrown a temper tantrum and dumped him. And maybe that was to be expected, too. She had been her father's darling, accustomed to having her own way. Her parents had given her anything she asked for, whether it was a new CD player or a diamond tennis bracelet. It was probably for the best that he and Cindy had broken up when they did. Even if they had somehow managed to stay together, he would never have been able to give her the kind of life she was used to, would never have been good enough for her. Hell, he didn't have anything to offer her. He never had, and he never would.

He stared at her reflection. He had been a fool, he thought, to believe she had loved him. And a bigger fool to think they could have worked things out. He was a poor Indian; she was Daddy's little princess. She had been raised in a big house; he had grown up on the reservation. She drove a BMW; he didn't even own a car. She went to college; he went to jail.

And yet, maybe he was selling himself short. Business at the ranch had picked up since he'd been here. In his own way, he was working to preserve his people's customs and traditions. Not only that, but he was helping Indian kids to be proud of their heritage.

Shaking off his memories, he went to the saddlebags and pulled out a can of tuna and a couple of French rolls.

He heard her footsteps coming up behind him. ''Can I help?''

He shook his head. ''I can do it.''

Cindy frowned at his back, puzzled by his curt tone. Last night he had treated her so tenderly she had almost believed he still cared.

He made two sandwiches, handed her one, along with a bottle of water.

His fingers brushed hers and sent frissons of awareness skittering up her arm. They ate in taut silence.

The tension between them grew more pronounced as the day wore on. Ethan paced the floor, restless as a caged animal. Cindy pretended to be oblivious to his presence, but she was acutely aware of his every move, his every breath. The fact that he was shirtless and barefoot only made it worse. He looked every inch the warrior he was, wild and untamed. She longed to touch him, to run her fingers through his hair, trace the corded muscles in his arms, run her palms over his chest. To feel his arms holding her tight, his mouth on hers…

The sound of the rain, which she usually found peaceful, grew increasingly annoying. By mid afternoon, the storm had passed by and the sun came out. That annoyed her, too. It meant they would be leaving soon, that the time they had shared would soon be over.

Too restless to sit any longer, she stood, intending to see if there was anything left to snack on in his saddlebags. Ethan was still pacing. He turned just then and ran into her. Instinctively, he reached for her to keep her from falling, and the next thing she knew, she was in his arms and he was kissing her, his mouth drinking from hers as if she were a pool of sparkling water and he was a man dying of thirst.

At first she was too startled to resist. And then, as he deepened the kiss, all thought of resistance fled and she leaned into him, her hands splaying across his broad back, her fingers kneading the muscles there. Her breasts were flattened against his chest. Tiny fires of desire ignited deep within her, the flames uncurling, stretching, engulfing her.

One of his hands cupped the back of her head, the other cupped her buttocks, drawing her up against him, letting her feel the full hard length of his arousal.

She moaned softly, confused by her quick response to a man she had vowed to hate and ignore for the rest of her life. But there was no way to ignore the heat of his kiss, or the yearnings of her own heart. The years seemed to fall away and she was sixteen again, being seriously kissed by a man for the first time.

She was breathless, her heart pounding like a Lakota war drum, when he finally broke the kiss. "Ethan…"

He stared down at her, looking as shaken as she felt. "Why, Cindy?" he asked, his voice husky. "Why didn't you return my calls? Answer my letters?"

She frowned. "What calls? What letters?"

He released her and took a step backward. "Don't play games with me, dammit. I called you day and night for a week. I wrote you a dozen letters. They all came back, unopened."

She blinked up at him. "There were no letters."

He ran a hand through his hair. "Dammit, don't lie to me!"

"I'm not lying. I called your mother the day after our fight. She told me you'd already left for Kansas City. I kept hoping you'd call me back, but you never did."

Ethan stared at her, wondering if she was telling him the truth. He wondered why his mother had never told him about Cindy's phone call, although he could guess. His mother hadn't been any happier about his dating a white girl than Cindy's folks had been about her dating him.

"Who did you talk to when you called?" she asked.

"Usually the maid. Your father answered a couple of times. He told me you didn't want to talk to me, that you never wanted to see me again."

She thought of that week before they had left for Europe. At her father's insistence, her mother had taken her shopping for their trip. They had left early every morning, often not coming home until after dark. Had her father deliberately planned it that way so she wouldn't be there to answer the phone or go through the mail? Cindy didn't want to think so, but looking back, she could see her father's fine hand in all of it.

He had been so sympathetic, so understanding. At the time, she had been too hurt to wonder at his sudden change of heart. Had it all been nothing but an act to throw her off guard and make her think he cared, when it had just been his way of getting Ethan out of her life once and for all?

Cindy shook her head, stunned by the thoughts running through her mind. "He couldn't," she murmured. "He wouldn't!" But she knew in her heart that he had.

"Well, he did, if what you say is true."

"You don't believe me? Why would I lie to you now?"

"Hell, I don't know." Going to the window, he stared into the distance. He had built a wall around his heart, refusing to let anyone in. Cindy had hurt him far worse than he had ever let on, and he had sworn he would never give anyone the power to hurt him like that again. But now... He thought about what she had said. There was no reason for her to lie to him at this late date. She had nothing to gain. And nothing to lose.

"What about Paul?" he asked.

"What about him?"

Ethan turned to face her, his gaze probing hers. "Did you sleep with him?"

She stared at him, stung that he would ask such a question. "Would it matter if I had?"

"You'd damn well better believe it."

"Well, I didn't, not that it's any of your business." She had never been tempted to sleep with Paul. When he had put pressure on her, saying everyone did it nowadays, she had told him she didn't care what everyone else was doing. She wanted to be married in a long white dress, and she wanted it to mean something. That was the truth, but not all of the truth. Her mother had taught her that her virginity was a precious gift to be given to the man she loved. And that man had been, and still was, Ethan Stormwalker. "Anyway, I don't know why it matters now."

Watching her closely, he said, "It matters."

Was it possible he was jealous? It sure sounded like it. Hope melted the ice around her heart. Was it possible he still cared? Did he mean...? "Ethan?"

He took a step toward her, but came to an abrupt halt when the cabin door swung open and Rudy barged in.

"Ethan! Damn, we've been looking everywhere for the two of you!" Rudy's gaze moved quickly over them. "You don't look any the worse for wear."

"We're fine," Ethan said. "Miss Wagner's horse threw her. She's okay," he added quickly. "Just a sprained ankle and a bump on the head. I thought it best not to try and make it to the ranch in the rain."

Rudy nodded. Removing his hat, he slapped it against his thigh, sending drops of water spraying across the floor. "I've got an extra mount with me." He resettled his hat on his head. "You two ready?"

Ethan nodded, grateful that Cindy would be riding away from the cabin sitting in the saddle and not draped over it.

It took but a few moments to gather up their gear. Ethan took a last look around to make sure they had everything, then followed Rudy and Cindy out of the shack.

It was slow going getting back to the ranch. The trail, slick with mud, was treacherous in some places and completely washed away in others. Wolf quartered back and forth ahead of them, his nose to the ground.

Between the ache in her head, the stress of navigating the trail and the things left unsettled with Ethan, Cindy was exhausted when they reached the ranch.

"Go tell my aunt we're back safe," Ethan told Rudy. "I'll see Miss Wagner to her cabin and look after her horse."

With a nod, Rudy rode toward the office.

When they reached her place, Ethan dismounted and lifted Cindy from the saddle. "You all right?" he asked.

"Yes, fine."

"Go get cleaned up and get some rest."

"Ethan…"

"We'll talk about it later."

She wasn't up to arguing with him. Right now, all she wanted was a hot bath, a good meal and a good night's sleep, in that order. "Thanks for coming after me."

With a nod, he swung onto his horse's back, then gathered up her horse's reins. "Stay off that ankle," he said. "I'll have one of the girls bring you a tray."

She smiled her thanks, watched him ride away until he was out of sight.

Compared to the shack, her cabin looked like a room at the Ritz. She filled the tub with hot water, added a generous amount of the vanilla-scented bubble bath she had picked up at the gift shop, and sank into a pool of liquid heaven.

Closing her eyes, she replayed the conversation she'd had with Ethan. How could her father have done such a despicable thing? All these years she might have spent with Ethan, wasted. She had compared every man she had dated to Ethan, and they had all come up short. Even Paul, though she had refused to admit it to herself until the moment she'd found herself standing beside him at the altar. Thank goodness she had come to her senses before it was too late!

Lying there immersed in bubbles, she searched her heart and knew she was perilously close to falling in love with Ethan Stormwalker all over again.

The next morning, Ethan stood in front of the buckskin's corral, his arms draped over the top rail, his thoughts not on breaking the stallion to ride, but on a black-haired girl with eyes as blue as a high country lake. Cindy. She had been young and immature when he first met her. Perhaps he'd known, even then, that their relationship was doomed to fail. But now…oh, Lord, she was a woman now, fully grown, beautiful and every bit as sweet as he remembered. Just thinking of her made his jeans feel two sizes too small.

And if she was telling the truth, her fiancé was out of the picture. Permanently. Damn. Ethan had resigned himself to living without her and now…now she was here, within reach. But nothing had really changed, he thought. Not one damn thing. He was still dirt poor with nothing to offer her, and she was still a rich girl who had everything she could ever want or need.

He slammed his fist against the rail. The noise sent the stallion running to the far side of the corral. The horse stood there staring at him, eyes wide, nostrils flared.

Muttering an oath, Ethan slipped through the corral rails. ''Easy, fella.'' He pulled a carrot out of his pocket and held it out. ''Come here, boy.''

The stallion watched him for several moments, ears twitching, and then moved cautiously toward him.

Ethan scratched the stallion's ears while the horse munched the carrot, then he dropped a bridle over the animal's head and led him around the corral. The buckskin followed docilely enough. In a day or two, Ethan would let him get used to the weight of a saddle on his back, and then the real job of breaking him to ride would begin.

But even as he put the horse through his paces, he was thinking of Cindy. He was going to dance tonight. Would she be in the audience? What more might have been said between them if Rudy hadn't burst into the cabin when he had? Ethan shook his head. Maybe he was reading more into what she had said than was there. He tried to tell himself that just because she hadn't meant to break up with him five years ago didn't mean she wanted him now. But she had sure kissed him like she meant it.

That thought stuck in his mind like a burr to a saddle blanket the rest of the day.

Ethan was dancing. Cindy told herself that wasn't the reason she had stopped at the lodge to look at the bulletin board, even though she knew it was. She had thought of him all last night, remembering the time they had spent together in the shack, wondering what might have happened between them if Rudy hadn't barged in when he did. She hadn't seen Ethan since this morning, when he'd stopped by to make sure she was all right. Now she had to decide whether to follow her heart and go watch him dance, or hide in her cabin and see if he would come looking for her.

Little tremors of excitement skittered through her every time she thought of what he had told her. He had called. He had sent her letters. He had asked Sally about her. But all that was in the past. How did he feel now? Did he still care, or was she reading more into his words and kisses than were really there?

She dressed with care that evening, donning a pair of black jeans and a short-sleeved black-and-white sweater she had picked up at the gift shop earlier that day. She applied her makeup with equal care, dabbed perfume behind her ears, on her wrists, in the cleft of her breasts. She brushed her hair until it gleamed like polished ebony, then let it fall loose down her back, because Ethan liked it that way.

She fidgeted all through dinner, too keyed up to eat much, too nervous to sit still.

Flo noticed it, of course.

"You all right, honey?" she asked, her voice filled with motherly concern.

"I'm fine," Cindy replied.

"We heard about your little ordeal. You're lucky you weren't badly hurt."

"Yes, very." She smiled, thinking of the time she had spent in the cabin with Ethan.

"Are you going to watch the dancing tonight?" Linda asked, her voice dreamy.

"Yes, I think so."

"Isn't he just too much?" the girl asked. "I mean, he's so sexy."

"Linda!" Flo exclaimed.

"Oh, Mom, get over it. You know it's true."

Flo looked at Cindy and they both laughed.

After dinner, Earl took Mary and Nancy up to the lodge to watch a movie. Cindy, Flo and Linda hurried toward the amphitheater.

They were early and got seats in the front row. Cindy wasn't sure if that was a good idea. She wasn't even sure if she wanted to be there. What if she was just building herself up for another letdown? Five years was a long time to be apart. Just because they'd shared a few kisses didn't mean he wanted to spend the rest of his life with her.

Her whole body was singing with anticipation when the drummers took their places around the big drum. Ethan had told her that, before they were played, drums were sometimes warmed over a fire to give them a richer, deeper tone.

He had told her much of the old ways of his people. She had often heard a note of regret in his voice, as if he wished he had lived in those days, when the Indians roamed the prairies and there were no white men west of the Missouri. It had been easy to imagine him as a warrior, wild and free on the plains, unfettered by the constraints of civilization, a stranger to clocks and conformity.

And it was easy to imagine it now as he took his place on the stage, tall and lithe, an eagle feather in his long black hair, zigzag streaks of black and white paint on his chest.

"My first dance tonight is the scalp dance," Ethan said. He spoke to the crowd, but he had eyes only for Cindy. "Scalping was not done merely out of cruelty or savagery or a need for vengeance. A scalp was a badge of honor, a tangible symbol of victory and of life itself. My people believed that the human spirit was somehow embodied in human hair. When a shaman wore human hair on his shirt, it represented all the people of his tribe. Parents who lost a child sometimes kept a lock of that child's hair. A warrior often presented a scalp to the relative of a man who had been killed in battle.

"In the old days, warriors danced to celebrate their victories. In those days, the men were joined by their mothers and sisters, who held the scalps aloft on a scalp pole."

The drummers had been drumming softly in the background, but now the sound and the tempo increased.

"In the old days, black face paint was worn by all who participated in the dance."

And now he began to dance, his body dropping into a crouch, his knees bent, his head high, his movements quick and warlike.

The rest of the dances—war dance, grass dance, traditional dance—blurred in Cindy's mind. She was aware of Ethan, only Ethan, his body moving, swaying, twisting and turning. She remembered once, long ago, when he had asked her to dance for him. She had been intrigued by the idea, but far too self-conscious to do what he asked.

His gaze rested on her face time and again and she knew he was dancing only for her, as he had once asked her to dance for him. *Someday,* he had said, *someday when you're secure in my love, you'll dance, just for me.*

Her body grew warm under his regard. She could feel the heat rising in her cheeks as she watched him, imagining herself entwined in his arms, their bodies writhing together in a dance all their own.

Just before the last dance, Flo leaned over and whispered, "Are you all right? You look a little flushed."

"I'm fine," Cindy replied, her voice husky.

She was feeling a little unsteady on her feet when Ethan

left the stage. The beating of the drum followed her out of the amphitheater, dogged her steps toward her cabin. And with every passing moment, she wondered if he would follow her. And what it would mean if he did.

Chapter Eight

Ethan gathered his gear and left the amphitheater, bound for his cabin. When he had first started dancing at the ranch, he had expressed his doubts to his aunt about performing for those who had no understanding or appreciation of the dances or what they meant. It had almost felt like selling out. But she had reminded him that it was an opportunity for him to share their beliefs with the whites, to help outsiders understand their customs, a way to narrow the gap between their two peoples. And she'd been right. Children often came up to him, wanting to know more about Native ways. Teenagers who had Indian blood but knew nothing of their heritage had told him that watching him dance filled them with a sense of pride in their ancestry. He had taken the time to teach some of them basic steps for some of the easier dances.

Wolf growled a soft welcome as he climbed the stairs to the porch. Hunkering down on his heels, Ethan spent a few moments scratching the dog's ears before going into the house to change clothes and wash the paint off his face and chest.

"So," he said, staring at his reflection in the mirror over the sink, "what now?"

Cindy had been there, front row center. Whenever he had looked her way, she had been watching him, her gaze seemingly riveted on him, her eyes alight. Her admiration filled him with a sense of exultation and he had poured his heart and soul into the steps. He had drawn upon the strength of his ancestors, asking them to infuse him with power, and had sensed their spirits hovering nearby. The drum had come alive for him then. He had felt its beat rise up through the soles of his moccasins, had heard the voice of the drum speaking to him as he danced. It had been, he mused, almost a spiritual experience, dancing for the only woman he had ever loved.

"What now?" he repeated.

He had never thought of himself as a coward. He had sought a vision. He had endured the sun dance. But this one small woman had the power to make him feel weak, helpless. He wasn't sure he had the fortitude to put his heart on the line a second time.

And yet even as doubts filled his mind, he was washing up, changing into a pair of jeans, shrugging into a clean T-shirt, running a comb through his hair.

Feeling like a still-wet-behind-the-ears sixteen-year-old boy about to embark on his first date, he left the cabin.

Cindy glanced out the window, then turned back to the book she was reading. Or trying to read, she thought, since she forgot the words as soon as she read them. She was waiting, she realized, waiting for Ethan to come calling.

She practically jumped out of her seat when she heard a rap on the door. It was him, she thought. It had to be him.

Taking a deep breath, she put the book aside, ran a hand over her hair, stood up and went to the door.

It was Ethan, looking more handsome than ever. Her heart seemed to turn over in her chest as she invited him in.

"It's a nice night," he said. "How would you like to take a walk?"

She agreed quickly, thinking it probably wasn't smart to be alone with him in her cabin.

They strolled along the riverbank, the tension high between them. She was acutely conscious of his nearness. He was very tall and very male and, as always, being with him made her feel deliciously female. Excitement rippled through her when his hand brushed against hers.

"You came to watch me tonight," he remarked after a while.

Cindy nodded. "I've always loved to watch you dance. You know that." She looked up at him. "Tonight was different somehow."

"What do you mean?"

"I'm not sure. It just felt different. I don't know how to explain it. It seemed more powerful, almost as if…"

He looked at her sharply. "Go on."

"As if you weren't alone up there."

Ethan came to an abrupt halt. Was it possible she had sensed the power of the Old Ones, felt their presence lingering nearby, as he had?

She stopped beside him, smiling sheepishly. "I guess that sounds silly."

"No." He took a deep breath, knowing his tongue would wither like a dead leaf if he didn't tell her how he felt.

"Ethan…" She reached out, her hand trembling as she laid it on his arm. "Is there any chance for us?"

"Cindy!"

"You don't know how sorry I am for what happened."

The words poured out of her, as if she was afraid that, if she didn't say them quickly, they would not get said. "I was so young. So foolish. I didn't mean what I said, but I was too proud to take it back and I...I guess I wanted to make you come to me and ask for my forgiveness. I realize now how wrong I was. I would have written back if I'd received your letters. I would have answered your phone calls. You have to believe me...."

"Shh, it's all right now. I believe you."

"Do you think we can try again?"

It was a chance he'd never thought to have. Life had been hell without her. Could he stand it if he lost her again? Could he live with himself if he didn't take the chance?

He ran his knuckles over her cheek.

"Ethan?" She looked up at him, waiting for his answer.

He whispered her name as he drew her into his arms, hugging her so tightly she thought her ribs might break. "You're sure," he said, "sure it's over between you and that bean counter?"

"I'm sure." She looked up at him, her gaze searching his. "Does that mean...is there hope for us then?" she asked tremulously.

"I've been living on it for the last five years," he replied, his voice gruff. "I don't ever want to lose you again."

With a sigh, she rested her cheek against his chest. "We'll make it work this time," she murmured.

He hadn't told her he loved her, but he would, she thought. He would. The words had never come easy to him; she couldn't blame him for being cautious now. But, oh, how she longed to hear them.

He kissed her and then took her hand in his and they walked in the moonlight, pausing now and then to share a kiss. There was so much to say, so much that needed to be said, but for now, it was enough that they were together.

Later that night, lying in bed unable to sleep, she thought about her life. It was nice having rich parents, never having to do without, never having to worry about a place to sleep or food to eat. And yet the money, the cars, the college education, the trip to Europe, all the things her father's money had bought her, had never really made Cindy happy. That fact had been brought home to her in a very real way when she broke up with Ethan. She had looked around her room, at all the expensive things in it, and realized how little it all meant if she didn't have Ethan to share it with.

When they had dated before, she had known Ethan had felt she was out of his league. On more than one occasion he had worried aloud that he would never be able to support her the way her father did. He had asked her time and again how she was going to feel if they got married and she could buy only what she needed and not everything she wanted. She had told him that wouldn't be a problem, but he had never truly believed her, and at that time, she wasn't sure she believed it, either.

Paul had given her things, too, but they had never made her happy, and it suddenly occurred to her that maybe that was what her mother had meant when she'd warned that Paul would never make her happy. No sooner had that thought crossed Cindy's mind than she found herself wondering if her mother was really happy with her father. Looking back, she remembered little comments her mom had made, times when she had wanted Jordan to come home from work early to spend more time with them. Time, she thought. It was the best gift of all, the one thing money couldn't buy.

With a sigh, she turned onto her side. She was here and Ethan was here, and they had all the time in the world to work things out.

* * *

Cindy pulled the covers over her head, but the knocking at the door went on and on. Groaning softly, she got out of bed, slipped on her robe and padded across the floor in her bare feet. Who on earth would be calling on her at this hour? Who but Ethan? she thought. Just thinking of him put a smile on her face as she opened the door.

"Good morning, Cyn."

She stared at the man on the stoop. He was clad in a long-sleeved Western shirt, jeans with a crease sharp enough to cut through timber, and a pair of squeaky clean boots. She closed her eyes a moment, certain she was dreaming, but when she opened them again, he was still there.

"Paul! What on earth are you doing here, of all places?"

"Aren't you going to invite me in?"

"What? Oh, of course." She took a step back. "Come in."

Closing the door, she took a deep breath, then sat down on the sofa, gesturing for him to join her. "What are you doing here?"

"What do you think?"

She shook her head. "I don't know."

"I came to take you home, of course. You've had time to come to your senses."

"I'm not ready to go home."

He smiled indulgently. "I thought you'd say that, so I got a room up at the lodge."

"You're staying here?" She frowned at him. "How did you find me?"

"I called your father."

"My father?"

Paul nodded. "It was easy enough to track you down."

"Oh?"

He smiled, obviously pleased with himself. "Your credit cards told us where you were. So." He slapped his knee. It was a gesture she had always hated. "Why don't you go and get dressed and I'll take you to breakfast. We need to talk." He glanced at her left hand. "Where's your ring?"

"I took it off. I was going to send it back to you."

"I see." There was no mistaking the displeasure in his eyes, or his voice.

"I'm sorry, Paul. I never should have let things go as far as they did."

"There's no point in rehashing the past. You made a mistake. I forgive you. Now let's go get something to eat."

He wasn't listening, she thought, but then, he never did. Deciding the quickest way to get rid of him was to do as he asked, she went into the bedroom to get dressed. Feeling contrary, she decided to take a long shower first, but eventually she had to go out and face him again.

He stood when she entered the room. "Ready?"

She nodded, and he followed her out the door. When they started walking, he took her arm, the way he always did.

She glanced from side to side as they strolled up the path toward the lodge, praying they wouldn't run into Ethan. She was in no mood to explain Paul's presence, nor was she sure, at this point, that Ethan would believe her. She had told him that it was over between her and her fiancé, and now Paul was here, acting as if he had every right to be.

She was just breathing a sigh of relief when she saw Ethan coming out of the lodge. Settling his hat on his head, he started down the stairs, only to come to an abrupt halt when he saw her. His gaze moved from her face to Paul's possessive grip on her arm and back again. And then, very deliberately, he turned his back on her and walked away.

She stared after him, praying that he would give her a chance to explain.

Ethan muttered every curse word he knew as he walked away from the lodge. Why had he ever believed it was over between Cindy and her rich boyfriend? He had no doubt that it was the long-suffering Paul walking beside her, come, no doubt, to take his runaway bride back home where she belonged. Damned tenderfoot, all duded up in brand-new Western clothes, as if a dandy like that would ever fit in here. Clothes might make the man in New York City, but it took more than new jeans and a fancy shirt to make a cowboy. Damn! Ethan should have known she'd come to her senses and call home. Why had he ever let himself believe there was hope for the two of them? She was like the sun, bright and out of reach, and he was just a dirt-poor Indian, fated to admire her from afar.

He swore again softly. At least he hadn't told her he still loved her. At least he hadn't made a complete fool of himself.

Stopping at the barn, he asked Rudy to take over the morning trail ride.

"You sick?" Rudy asked.

"No, I'm just not in the mood to put up with a lot of greenhorns. Can you cover for me?"

"Sure, no problem," Rudy replied. "Alex and I will look after those city slickers."

"Obliged. I'll take the second bunch out for you this afternoon."

Rudy gave him a thumbs-up. "Works for me."

With a nod, Ethan jogged along the river trail that led to his cabin. Plucking his lariat off a fence post, he roped the buckskin, then tied the horse to the snubbing post in the center of the corral. He stood there for a moment, talking softly to the stallion, stroking his neck until the animal quieted. Moving quickly and efficiently, Ethan slipped a hackamore over the horse's head, smoothed a blanket in place and cinched the saddle down tight. Removing the rope, he took up the reins and swung into the saddle.

The stallion stood there a moment, his whole body quivering, before he took off across the corral, bucking. He made a swift turn at the last minute, almost scraping Ethan out of the saddle, before racing back across the corral, bucking and crow-hopping.

Ethan threw back his head, the Lakota victory cry rising in his throat as the stallion broke into a gallop and then gradually slowed to a trot, a walk.

Leaning forward, Ethan patted the stud's neck. ''That's enough for today, boy.''

''Bravo!''

Ethan looked over his shoulder to find Cindy perched on the top rail of the corral. ''What the hell are you doing here?''

She bit down on her lower lip, hurt by his tone and the accusation in his deep gray eyes. ''Do you want me to leave?''

Ethan glanced around. ''Where's Mr. Moneybags?''

''He had to make a couple of phone calls.''

Ethan grunted softly as he rode toward her. Checking on his stocks, no doubt. ''What do you want?''

''Ethan, don't do this, please.''

''Do what?''

''Don't shut me out. I can't bear it.''

''You said it was over between the two of you, yet here he is. Are you gonna tell me it's just a coincidence?''

''I can't help it if he came looking for me.''

''Go back to him. There's nothing for you here.''

''You can't mean that!'' she exclaimed. ''Not after last night…''

''Cindy, let it go. I'm no good for you. I never was. Las

night, being so close to you, I..." He shrugged. "Things will never work out between us, and you know it."

"That's not true!"

"Isn't it? Look at me. I don't have anything to offer you."

She looked at him mutely, the hurt in her eyes ripping his insides to shreds.

She was too close. It would be so easy to reach for her, to pull her into the saddle. And then what? He clenched his hands into tight fists to keep from reaching for her. Seeing her with her supposed ex had made it clearer than ever that Ethan wasn't good enough for her. Cindy and her young man looked as though they were made for each other, as though they had been cut from the same cloth, while he... Ethan snorted softly. She was silk and satin and he was cheap cotton, and they would never look like they belonged together.

"Hell," he muttered, "I don't even own a car."

"You can have one of mine." It was the wrong thing to say. She knew it the moment the words were out, but it was too late to take them back.

"Go home, Cindy."

She stared at him, fighting back the tears stinging her eyes. She wanted to beg him to reconsider, wanted to beat her fists on that solid masculine chest and tell him she loved him and no one else, that he would never find anyone else to love him the way she did. But pride, that same damnable pride that had come between them before, trapped the words in her throat. She had told him last night that she wanted to be with him, and what good had it done?

Wrapping her dignity around her like a cloak, she climbed down from the rail and then, with her head high and her shoulders back, made her way toward the river trail. Only when she was out of his sight did she let the tears come.

* * *

Hands clenched on the reins, Ethan stared after her, afraid he had just made the biggest mistake of his life. Letting her go hurt like the devil, but better now than later, he decided. Oh, sure, she might think she still loved him, and maybe she did, in her way. But after a year or two of living with him and making do on his meager salary, she would come to her senses. He couldn't give her a big house or servants. He couldn't afford to give her an unlimited expense account or vacations in Europe. And he for damn sure wasn't going to let *her* support *him!* No, better to end it now before it began. In the long run, she would realize he had been right. Hell, she'd probably thank him.

Dismounting, he unsaddled the stallion and gave him a good rubdown. When that was done, he turned the horse loose in the corral. The stallion shook his head, then trotted off to stand in the shade.

Leaving the corral, Ethan removed his hat and dipped his head in the horse trough. Shaking the water from his hair, he replaced his hat and then swore under his breath. Dammit, why had he let her go? She was the best thing that had ever happened to him, the only thing in his life that had ever mattered. And yet what did he have to offer her? Life on a dude ranch, in a four-room cabin that wasn't his? A half-wild mustang? A prison record?

Muttering an oath, he dragged the hose over to the corral and filled the water barrel inside. Letting her go had been the right choice, the only choice.

"All right," Paul said, rubbing his hands together. "What would you like to do?"

"No more phone calls?" Cindy asked with a trace of sarcasm. She had returned to her cabin to find Paul waiting for her. She didn't know how he'd gotten inside, but he'd made himself at home. The radio was playing; there was a coffee cup on the table.

"Nope. I'm all yours."

She closed her eyes, thinking how happy she would be to hear those words on Ethan's lips. "Paul, it won't work. It's over between us."

"Now, Cyn..."

"Listen to me! Can't you for once just listen to me? I don't love you. I never did."

He looked momentarily taken aback, and then he smiled indulgently. "Cyn, you know you don't mean that."

It was like talking to her father, she thought. Like Paul, Jordan Wagner heard only what he wanted to hear.

She grabbed her hat. "I'm going riding."

"I'll go with you."

"Whatever." This should be good, she thought. To her knowledge, Paul had never been on a horse. At least Ethan wouldn't be there to watch Paul make a fool of himself.

When they reached the stable, the wrangler was already helping the other riders to mount.

"Do you have room for two more?" Cindy asked.

"Yes, ma'am."

She smiled as Alex led a pair of horses out of the barn. He quickly saddled them, helped Cindy mount a pretty little chestnut mare, then went to adjust the stirrups for Paul.

"All right, folks," the wrangler said. "Here comes your guide now."

Cindy turned, expecting to see Rudy, then felt her stomach turn over when she saw Ethan ride into view.

His gaze met hers. Heat sizzled between them. He might not want to spend his life with her, she thought bitterly, but he wanted her, wanted her just as much as she wanted him. Had anyone walked between them just then, she was sure they would have been burned to ash.

. With an effort, Ethan drew his gaze from Cindy's. His eyes narrowed ominously when he saw Paul at her side, and then he took his place at the head of the group.

Cindy stared after him. "This day just keeps getting better and better," she muttered, and clucking to the mare, she took her place near the back of the line.

Chapter Nine

Some perverse devil made Ethan choose one of the more difficult trails through the back country. He let the wrangler who rode with him take the lead, and he fell back to the rear. After the first five minutes, he knew Cindy's wealthy boyfriend had never been on a horse. Listening to that same perverse devil, he called for a trot. Mr. Moneybags bounced up and down in the saddle like popcorn in a pan. But it was Cindy who more often caught his eye, Cindy who rode with a natural seat and who tried, without success, to instruct her fiancé. Ethan smothered a grin. The man was going to be sore from head to foot by the end of the ride.

Cindy felt her temper rise as they crossed the river and started up a long winding trail. This wasn't the easy trail they had taken before. It was Ethan's doing, she was sure of it.

Hoping to make him jealous, she reached over and touched Paul's arm. "Are you okay?"

He looked at her and smiled wanly. "F-fine. A little...bumpy...isn't it?"

Cindy pulled back on the reins, easing her horse into a walk. Paul's horse also slowed. In minutes, the rest of the group was out of sight around a bend in the trail.

"Excuse me, Miss Wagner," said a deep voice behind them. "You and your friend will have to keep up with the others."

Pasting a sugary sweet smile on her face, Cindy turned to Ethan. "I'm so sorry," she said, "but I just can't seem to keep up that pace." She stood in the stirrups and rubbed her fanny. "I'm getting *so* sore."

Ethan glared at her, knowing as well as she did that she was lying.

She glared back, daring him to call her bluff.

Putting his fingers to his lips, Ethan whistled shrilly. It was, she knew, a signal to the wrangler to slow down until the rest of the group caught up.

Smiling smugly, Cindy settled back in the saddle and clucked to her mount. She was aware of Ethan's furious gaze burning into her back.

They caught up with the other riders a short time later. Most of them had dismounted and were sitting in the shade alongside a shallow stream.

"Everything okay?" the wrangler called as they rode into view.

"Just fine," Ethan answered.

Cindy bit back a grin at the edge in his voice.

"Okay, ladies and gents," the wrangler said. "Let's hit the trail."

Cindy deliberately lagged again, letting the other riders get ahead. She did it knowing it would irritate Ethan, though she wasn't sure why she wanted to except that she was mad as hell at him. As if it was her fault Paul had shown up at the ranch! She had told Ethan she was through with Paul, and she was. But did he believe her? Oh, no, and what was worse, he refused to let her explain.

Some of her annoyance waned as they rode through a wide meadow ringed with trees and studded with flowers. This really was God's country, she thought, feeling the beauty of it soothe her anger.

The rest of the ride proved uneventful. It was time for lunch when they returned to the ranch. Paul insisted on eating with her, and since she didn't really want to eat alone, she didn't object.

After lunch, they played horseshoes with Flo and her husband. When Ethan walked by, Cindy laughed and pretended to be having the time of her life. He scowled when he looked at her, and when he was gone, she sat down on the bench, wondering what she was trying to prove. It was foolish to antagonize him, she thought, yet she couldn't seem to help herself.

Later, the four of them went up to the bar for drinks, and then Cindy excused herself to go and get cleaned up for dinner.

Standing under the shower, with the hot water soothing the ache of two hours in the saddle, she found her thoughts turning to Ethan as surely as night followed day. Stubborn man! They had just started to find their way back to each other and now this! Darn Paul. His timing couldn't have been worse!

Wrapping her hair in a towel, she stepped out of the shower. She put on her robe, then began to blow dry her hair, wondering how she could avoid Paul for the rest of the night.

As it turned out, it wasn't a problem. He called her on the phone, saying he was too sore to get out of the tub and he would see her at breakfast in the morning.

She hung up the phone, then twirled around the room, feeling suddenly light and carefree. The evening stretched ahead of her, a gift to be savored.

She finished drying her hair, then put on the rose-colored

sundress she had bought in town. Slipping on her sandals, she left her cabin and walked up to the lodge to see what events were scheduled for the evening. The agenda on the bulletin board revealed that there was going to be a canasta tournament in the game room and a Disney movie in the rec room. She wasn't in the mood for either and she was checking to see what else was being offered when she heard the familiar sound of drumming.

Following the crowd headed toward the amphitheater, she hurried to catch up to Linda Petersen.

"Hi, Miss Wagner," Linda said.

"Hi. What's going on?"

"Haven't you heard? The movie projector broke, so Mrs. Donovan asked Stormwalker to fill in. Isn't that exciting? Don't you just love him!"

"Yes," Cindy murmured, following Linda down the aisle, where they found two seats near the front on the side. "I do."

The lights dimmed as the drumming grew louder. A hush fell over the crowd as Ethan walked into view. On this night he wore only a brief wolfskin breechclout and moccasins. A single eagle feather adorned his hair; a single slash of black paint bisected his left cheek.

Cindy leaned forward, her whole being focused on Ethan. She didn't hear the introduction or anything else. All she saw was Ethan looking more wild, more dangerous, more blatantly sexy than ever before. Desire unfolded within her as she watched him dance. His steps were intricate, filled with an energy and an anger that was palpable. He drew a knife from a sheath on his belt. Lamplight glinted on the blade as he slashed at an invisible enemy, and she knew the enemy was Paul. His steps quickened as he destroyed his enemy, and then he threw back his head and the fierce victory cry of the Lakota filled the air. The sound was like nothing she had ever heard before and sent shivers down her spine.

Applause filled the amphitheater when he finished dancing.

Ethan stood there, his body sheened with sweat, his dark eyes alight with an inner fire as he looked out over the audience. Excitement rippled through Cindy when his gaze came to rest on her face.

He might be angry, she thought. He might think he could walk away from her and not look back, but she knew, in that moment, that she had the power to win him back.

Breathing heavily, Ethan stared at Cindy. She looked as pretty as a prairie flower in a pink sundress that emphasized her golden tan and complimented her dark hair. She was looking at him as if he was the only person in the amphitheater, the only person in the world. He had noticed immediately that Mr. Moneybags was not with her. He would have liked to believe that the man had gone home, but he'd checked up at the lodge earlier and Mr. Paul VanDerHyde was still in residence. Ethan grinned inwardly. The only other explanation for the man's absence was that he was too sore from the long trail ride that afternoon to leave his cabin.

The soft drumming began again. Ethan's gaze met Cindy's and then he began to dance once more, always aware that she was watching. Did she know he danced just for her, that he had eyes only for her?

He finished the dance and then, needing to take a break, he sat down and waited for the applause to die away. When he again had the crowd's attention, he began to speak.

"For hundreds of years, before my people learned to read and write, we handed our stories and legends down from father to son. The story I'm about to tell you is one I heard from my grandmother when I was a young boy on the reservation.

"Long, long ago, when the world was young and people had not come out yet, no flowers bloomed on the prairie. Only grasses and dull, greenish-gray shrubs grew there. Earth felt very sad because her robe lacked brightness and beauty.

"'I have many beautiful flowers in my heart,' Earth said to herself. 'I wish they were on my robe. Blue flowers like the clear sky in fair weather, white flowers like the snow of winter, brilliant yellow ones like the sun at midday, pink ones like the dawn of a spring day—all these are in my heart. I am sad when I look at my dull robe, all gray and brown.'

"A sweet little pink flower heard Earth talking. 'Do not be sad, Mother Earth. I will go upon your robe and beautify it.'

"So the little pink flower came up from the heart of the Earth Mother to beautify the prairies. But when the Wind Demon saw her, he growled, 'I will not have that pretty flower on my playground.'

"He rushed at her, shouting and roaring, and blew out her life. But her spirit returned to the heart of Mother Earth.

"When other flowers gained courage to go forth, one after another, Wind Demon killed them also. And their spirits returned to the heart of Mother Earth.

"At last Prairie Rose offered to go. 'Yes, sweet child,' said Earth, 'I will let you go. You are so lovely and your breath so fragrant that surely the Wind Demon will be charmed by you. Surely he will let you stay on the prairie.'

"So Prairie Rose made the long journey up through the dark ground and came out on the drab prairie. As she went, Mother Earth said in her heart, 'Oh, I do hope that Wind Demon will let her live.'

"When Wind Demon saw her, he rushed toward her, shouting, 'She is pretty, but I will not allow her on my playground. I will blow out her life.'

"So he rushed on, roaring and drawing his breath in strong gusts. As he came closer, he caught the fragrance of Prairie Rose. "Oh, how sweet!' he said to himself. 'I do not have it in my heart to blow out the life of such a beautiful maiden with so sweet a breath. She must stay here with me. I must make my voice gentle, and I must sing sweet songs. I must not frighten her away with my awful noise.'

"So Wind Demon changed. He became quiet. He sent gentle breezes over the prairie grasses. He whispered and hummed little songs of gladness. He was no longer a demon.

"Then other flowers came up from the heart of the Earth Mother, up through the dark ground. They made her robe, the prairie, bright and joyous. Even Wind came to love the blossoms growing among the grasses of the prairie. And so the robe of Mother Earth became beautiful because of the loveliness, the sweetness and the courage of the Prairie Rose.

"Sometimes Wind forgets his gentle songs and becomes loud and noisy. But his loudness does not last long. And he does not harm a person whose robe is the color of the Prairie Rose.''

Charmed by the tale, the audience applauded as Ethan gained his feet. He sent a last look in Cindy's direction, and then he left the stage.

Cindy stared down at her dress. The color was the deep pink of a prairie rose. She frowned, wondering if there had been a hidden message in the story he had told.

Chapter Ten

Ethan paced the floor most of that night, trying to convince himself that he didn't need Cynthia Wagner. He had survived the last five years without her; he could get through the next five just as well.

Going to the window, he stared out into the night. Who was he trying to kid? He had been trying to get over her for five years, three months and six days, and he hadn't managed it yet. In all that time, not a day had gone by without him thinking about her, wondering where she was, what she was doing. Why the hell hadn't she married Mr. Moneybags? Even though she would still be in Ethan's thoughts, still a temptation, at least she would be untouchable. And even though it would hurt like the devil knowing she belonged to someone else, at least he would know she was out of reach. Maybe then he'd be able to move on. And maybe he'd win the lottery. And maybe the government would return the Black Hills to the Lakota.

Knowing he was never going to be able to get any sleep, he left the cabin. Wolf crawled out from under the porch and padded at Ethan's heels as he walked to the corral. The stallion snorted softly at their approach.

"Wolf, down," Ethan said quietly.

Whining softly, the dog dropped to his belly, his head resting on his paws.

Ethan draped his arms over the top rail. Sometimes, like now, he thought about just giving up and going back to the reservation, living from allotment check to allotment check. He had a lot of old friends there. They could go hunting and fishing, spend their evenings sitting outside chewing the fat. He could move in with his cousins. They'd be happy to see him, happy to put him up for as long as he wanted to stay.... Yet even as he considered it, he knew he wouldn't go. Dorothea needed his help here, and he liked working on the ranch. He was his own boss, more or less. He had a place of his own, plenty of time off, the opportunity to dance as often or as little as he liked.

But that wasn't the only reason. Visiting at Pine Ridge Reservation always filled him with a sense of despair. Jobs were scarce. A high percentage of kids were high school dropouts. The suicide rate was high, as was the rate of infant mortality and diabetes. There were few paved roads, few businesses; there were still conflicts between the mixed bloods and the full-bloods, between progressive Indians who wanted to embrace the ways of the white man, and traditional Indians who wanted to preserve and emphasize the old ways. Back in the mid-seventies, those tensions had erupted in a bloody battle at Wounded Knee, where another bloody battle had taken place over a hundred years ago.

His cousin, Joseph Little Eagle, likened living on the reservation to living in a concentration camp.

With a sigh of exasperation, Ethan grabbed the hackamore off the post where he had left it the day before. There was no point in lamenting the past or thinking about Cindy and what might have been.

Ducking inside the corral, he dropped the hackamore over the stallion's head, then swung onto his bare back. He spent an hour teaching the horse to rein right and left, make flying lead changes, to back up. To Ethan's delight, the animal was smart and quick.

Finally reining the stallion to a halt, he leaned forward to stroke his neck. They had both had a good workout, he thought. Maybe now he could get some sleep.

Dismounting, he slipped the hackamore off the buckskin's head. Snorting softly, the horse trotted to the far side of the corral. Hanging the hackamore over the post again, Ethan ducked through the rails.

Wolf stood up, a low growl rumbling in his throat as he stared into the darkness.

"Something out there, boy?" Ethan asked.

"You're up late."

Cindy's voice impaled him with a shaft of sweet hot desire. Taking a deep breath, he turned slowly to face her. "So are you."

"I couldn't sleep."

"Try a glass of warm milk."

She glanced at the stallion. "It doesn't seem to work for you."

"I don't like milk. What do you want, Cindy?"

"The same thing I've always wanted." Her gaze met his. "You."

"It's never going to work. Why can't you accept that?"

"Because I'm nothing but a spoiled rich girl used to getting her own way."

He flinched as she tossed his own words back at him. "Even spoiled rich girls have to learn to accept defeat."

"I'm not defeated."

"Well, I am."

"Damn you, Ethan Stormwalker. I know you still care for me. Why won't you fight for me?"

"Honey, I don't have any ammunition."

"Tell me you don't care." She took a step toward him. "Tell me that I don't mean anything to you, that you haven't missed me as much as I've missed you." Another step. "Tell me I'm not the reason you're out here, unable to sleep."

"Dammit, Cindy…"

Closing the distance between them, she placed her hand on his chest. He wasn't wearing a shirt and his skin was warm beneath her fingertips. She could feel the rapid beating of his heart, feel his breath on her face.

"Tell me, Ethan, and I'll go away and you'll never have to see me again."

She was close. Too close. And he wanted her more than he wanted to see another sunrise.

"This doesn't mean anything," he said, his voice rough as sandpaper, and then he dragged her body up against his and kissed her. There was no tenderness in his kiss, no softness in his caress. His mouth plundered hers boldly, his tongue dueling with hers. He kissed her until she couldn't breathe, couldn't think, until her body was on fire and there was nothing in the world but Ethan, his arms locked around her, his body rigid and pulsing with desire.

He released her abruptly and took a step backward. "Go home, Cindy. You don't belong here. You never will."

She looked up at him, her eyes like dark bruises in her face, and then she turned and walked away.

She had tried and she had failed. Blinded by her tears, Cindy made her way back to her cabin. Inside, she hit her knee against a chair while she fumbled for the light switch, but the pain in her leg was nothing compared to the ache in her heart.

He said he didn't want her, but she couldn't believe it.

Refused to believe it. He hadn't kissed her like he didn't
want her.

She sank down on the sofa and closed her eyes. Why did
she have to come here and see him again? Why did it have
to hurt so badly? Maybe her father was right. Maybe she
should marry Paul. They came from the same background.
They were comfortable with each other. He was at ease at
the opera and the ballet. He had an M.B.A. from the Whar-
ton School of Business. His parents liked her; her parents
liked him. He would never dance just for her, or walk barefoot with her along the beach at night. He would never give
her an eagle feather. He would never break her heart....

Anger surged up within her. Why was she sitting here
feeling sorry for herself? She was young. She was single.
She was smart. She wasn't bad looking. If Ethan was too
blind to realize it, that was his loss! She didn't need him...!
But she did. And that quickly, her anger withered and died.
She was one other thing, she thought, grinning. She was
tenacious and stubborn and used to getting what she wanted.
And she wanted Ethan Stormwalker. And she meant to have
him. She had told Ethan she wasn't defeated, and she
wasn't.

"I'll get him back," she said, and then grinned again,
thinking she sounded just like Scarlett O'Hara talking about
Rhett Butler. "You and me, Scarlett," she murmured,
"Only I intend to win!"

Paul was at her door bright and early the next morning.
Dressed in a crisp plaid shirt, a string tie, a pair of Levi's
and boots so shiny she could see her face in them, he looked
exactly like the greenhorn he was.

"Hi, Cyn," he said with a smile. "Ready for breakfast?"

There was no point in refusing to go with him. She was
hungry and she had to eat. She brightened a little, thinking

there was a good chance they might bump into Ethan up at the lodge.

And bump into him was just what she did. He was coming out of the dining room as they were going in, only Cindy was looking at Paul and didn't see him.

Ethan grabbed her by the arm to steady her. "Excuse me, Miss Wagner." His voice was cool, but she saw the heat in his eyes when he looked at her.

"My fault," she replied, her voice equally cool. "Mr. Stormwalker, I don't believe you've met my friend, Paul VanDerHyde." She emphasized the word *friend.* "Paul, this is Ethan. You remember him? He was our guide on the trail ride the other day."

"Yes, of course," Paul said. He did not offer his hand to the other man.

Ethan nodded in acknowledgment, his own hands clenched at his sides.

Cindy glanced from one man to the other. They were sizing each other up like two dogs about to fight over a bone. The silence built until it was uncomfortable.

"Nice to meet you, Mr. Stormwalker. Come along, Cyn," Paul said, and taking her by the arm, he led her past Ethan into the dining room.

They found a table beside a window and sat down. The waitress brought coffee and took their order.

"Who is that man?" Paul asked when the waitress had moved away from the table.

"He works here. You know that."

"Yes, but who is he? What is he to you?"

Her senses went on red alert. "What do you mean?"

"You know him, don't you?" He held up his hand, cutting her off. "And I don't mean because he works here."

"I met him before, yes."

"Stop being so damned evasive. Who is he, Cyn? What does he mean to you?"

"Everything," she replied quietly. "He means everything to me."

Paul stared at her as if she had just grown another head. "You're in love with *him?* An Indian trail guide?" He shook his head and then laughed. "Dammit, Cyn, you had me going for a minute there!"

"It's true, Paul. I'm in love with him."

"I see." His eyes grew cold and hard. "So, he's the reason you left me looking like a fool at the altar?"

"I'm sorry."

"And how does he feel about you?"

"That's none of your business. In fact, none of this is any of your business."

"The hell it isn't! I can't believe you left me for some…some cowboy!"

Cindy glanced around the dining room. Several of the diners at nearby tables were looking in their direction.

Paul noticed it, too, and immediately lowered his voice. "I asked you a question, and I want an answer. How does he feel about you?"

"Why don't you ask him?" she replied. Rising, she tossed her napkin on the table and walked out of the dining room.

Afraid that Paul might follow her, Cindy began to run as soon as she got outside. Ducking around the side of the lodge, she headed for the stream and splashed across to the other side. She ran until her sides ached and her lungs burned, and then she sank down under a tree and fell back on the grass to catch her breath.

Men! She remembered a greeting card she had read that said, if they could put one man on the moon, why couldn't they put them all there? At times like these, she agreed wholeheartedly! One good thing might have come out of it, though. She didn't think Paul would bother her anymore.

Lying there in the shade, she felt strangely detached from everything and everyone. The sky was a clear azure blue, the air was warm, fragrant with the scents of grass and trees and wildflowers. High overhead, an eagle made lazy circles.

Lakota country, she thought. She had studied the Plains tribes in college, fascinated by their beliefs and customs, always thinking of Ethan, always imagining him living in the Old West. She closed her eyes. It was so easy to picture him there....

She was riding across a vast prairie under an endlessly blue summer sky. There was nothing to be seen in any direction for miles and miles, yet she wasn't afraid. She rode on, enjoying the touch of the sun on her face, her gaze searching, endlessly searching.

The day wore on, the shadows lengthened, and still she rode onward, ignoring her growing weariness, the hunger and thirst that were making themselves known. She couldn't stop. She had to find him.

And then he was there, riding over the crest of a hill, his skin the color of sun-warmed copper, his long black hair shining in the silver light of a lover's moon.

She drew her horse to a halt, watching as he rode toward her, tall and proud, a warrior without equal.

With a joyous cry, she fell into his arms, sobbing his name as he held her close, promising that she would never leave him again. Never...

Cindy woke with a smile on her face. It was a sign, she thought, a sign that he would be hers.

Paul was waiting for her when she returned to her cabin.

Cindy took a deep breath, prepared to do battle. "What do you want?"

He had been standing with one arm behind his back. Now he brought it forward and handed her a bouquet of yellow daisies. "I brought you a peace offering."

She hesitated a moment before accepting them. "Thank you, but this doesn't change anything. It's over between us, Paul."

He nodded. "I understand, but there's no reason we can't be friends, is there?" He smiled disarmingly. "No reason why we can't spend a few days together as long as I'm here."

"Paul…"

"I think you owe it to me, don't you?" As though sensing she was about to argue, he said, "One day and one night," he said. "That's all I'm asking for. Starting tomorrow."

"And then what?"

"And then I'm gone."

She looked down at the flowers in her hands. She didn't feel she owed him anything, but he wasn't asking for much, just one day. And maybe she did owe him something for the way she had treated him. And what could one day hurt, as long as he knew it was over between them? "All right."

"Good. Oh, there's a dance tonight up at the lodge. Maybe I'll see you there."

"Maybe."

He started to say something and apparently thought better of it.

"Thank you for the flowers. They're lovely."

"They pale next to you."

"Paul…"

Leaning forward, he brushed a kiss across her cheek. "A day and a night," he reminded her. "I'll come by for you tomorrow morning."

Chapter Eleven

Cindy stood in front of the closet, a towel wrapped around her body. She frowned as she tried to decide whether she wanted to put on her sundress and go up to the lodge or slip into her nightgown and hide out in her room.

What should she do?

Ethan didn't want to see her, but she very much wanted to see him.

Paul wanted to see her, but she didn't want to see him.

Deciding she wanted to see Ethan more than she didn't want to see Paul, she let the towel drop to the floor. And then, with a defiant toss of her head, she reached for her bright yellow sundress. Ethan Stormwalker would see her whether he wanted to or not.

The lodge was crowded when she arrived, mostly with adult couples, though there were a few teenagers here and there. She assumed most of the other kids were in the game room. She saw two of the Native drummers standing together in a corner, along with three Lakota women. Wives and girlfriends, she supposed. She saw Linda Petersen sitting at a small table. Cindy grinned, certain that Linda was there in hopes of seeing Ethan.

A three-piece band was playing an old Brooks and Dunn song. Cindy noticed the third Indian drummer was playing the guitar. She wondered briefly if the men were related to Ethan and Dorothea.

Flo and Earl danced by. Flo waved when she saw her and Cindy waved back, and then walked over to Linda's table. "Hi, mind if I sit down?"

"Of course not," Linda said. "How are you, Miss Wagner?"

"Fine, and call me Cindy. Your folks look good out there."

Linda rolled her eyes. "I guess so." She glanced around the room. "Do you think Stormwalker will be here?"

"I don't know."

"Even if he does come, I don't suppose he'd dance with me," Linda said morosely. "He probably thinks I'm just a kid."

Before Cindy could form an answer, Paul walked up to their table.

"Evening, Cyn. Care to dance?"

Linda looked at Cindy and winked. It was easy enough to read the girl's mind. She was thinking Paul was mighty cute, which Cindy had to admit was true. He was wearing a pair of cream-colored trousers and a brown pullover shirt that perfectly complimented his brown eyes.

He held out his hand. "Shall we?"

"I guess so," Cindy said. Ignoring his hand, she followed him onto the dance floor.

Paul drew her into his arms. They had always danced well together and he twirled her effortlessly around the floor. She knew they made a striking couple—Paul with his summer-blond hair and fair skin, she with her black hair and olive complexion. But even as they danced, her gaze was skimming the room, searching for a tall man with hair as black as her own. Would he be here tonight? Or would he stay away, hoping to avoid her?

"Remember that night in Sarasota when we danced on the beach?" Paul said.

"Yes." It had been shortly after they became engaged. She'd still had stars in her eyes then, still been caught up in the newness and the excitement of the whirlwind that was Paul VanDerHyde.

"It can be like that again, Cyn."

They'd had good times, she thought, at least in the beginning, when she had thought she was more important to him than making money, before she realized he was making all her decisions, gradually changing her from the woman she was into the one he wanted her to be.

The dance ended and they left the dance floor. "I'm going to get something to drink," Paul said. "Would you like something?"

"Yes, thanks."

She wandered back over to the Petersen table to wait for Paul. Flo was sitting there with Linda.

"Who's the new man?" Flo asked.

Cindy sat down across from Linda. "An old boyfriend, actually," she said. "We were engaged."

Flo's eyebrows rose. "Oh?"

"Yes. We broke up not long ago."

"And he came here after you," Linda said, looking dreamy-eyed. "Oh, that's so romantic!"

"I suppose it would be," Cindy said, "if I still cared. But…"

The words died in her throat as she saw Ethan on the dance floor. He was holding a pretty redheaded woman in his arms; a young woman clad in a pair of skintight black jeans, a red spandex tank top and a smile that said "Take me, I'm yours."

Cindy recognized her as one of the waitresses from the dining room. She stared at the two of them, a wave of jealousy unlike anything she had ever known before flooding through her.

She clenched her hands into tight fists as Paul stepped into her line of vision.

"All they have is soft drinks and lemonade," he said, placing a tall frosty glass in front of her.

She nodded.

Paul looked at Flo and Linda, and when Cindy didn't introduce him, he smiled at them and held out his hand. "Hello. I'm Paul VanDerHyde, Cindy's fiancé."

"Ex-fiancé," Cindy muttered, but no one was listening.

"Flo Petersen," Flo said, shaking his hand. "And this is my daughter Linda. Oh, and this is my husband, Earl," she added as he approached the table.

Paul sat down and was soon engrossed in a discussion about the stock market with Earl.

Flo rapped Cindy on the arm. "Are you all right, honey?"

"What? Oh, yes, fine. I was just…just…" She swallowed hard, determined not to cry.

Flo regarded her curiously, but didn't pry. A few minutes later, the lights dimmed and the strains of a soft slow ballad filled the room.

Paul stood up and offered Cindy his hand. "Shall we?"

She was about to refuse when she saw Ethan lead the red-haired woman onto the floor. "Yes," she said, and forcing a smile, she stood and moved into Paul's arms.

She knew the moment Ethan saw her. Time seemed to stand still as his gaze met hers. She was surprised that the electricity that hummed between them didn't send sparks shooting across the room.

Ethan laughed at something his partner said and the sight filled Cindy with such pain she thought she might collapse right there, on the dance floor. Instead, she stiffened her spine, smiled up at Paul and then, leaning closer, she kissed him.

Paul was startled, but not so startled that he didn't take advantage of the situation and kiss her back.

When she opened her eyes and glanced around, Ethan and the waitress were gone.

She wasn't sure how she got through the rest of the evening. She remembered making small talk with Flo and Linda while Paul and Earl talked about the stock market and the interest rate and which company built the best truck, Ford or Chevy.

When the dance was over, they bid the Petersens good-night and Paul walked her back to her cabin.

"So," he said, "was that kiss for my benefit or his?"

A wave of telltale heat swept into her cheeks, making her grateful for the darkness.

"You don't have to answer that," Paul said, his voice tinged with anger. "I don't think I'd like the answer." He took her hand in his and kissed it, his lips cool. "I'll see you in the morning."

Ethan shoved his hands in the pockets of his Levi's, wondering what the devil had possessed him to ask Millie if she'd like to go for a walk. He didn't feel like making small talk about the ranch, or sidestepping her veiled hints to spend the night with her. It wasn't that he didn't find her attractive, it was just that she was the wrong woman at the wrong time. He muttered a mild oath, wondering what the right woman was doing. Was she walking in the moonlight with her supposed former fiancé? Kissing him good-night? Making plans for another wedding?

Dammit!

Millie smiled up at him. "Did you say something?"

"No."

"You seem sort of far away. Is something bothering you? You can tell me, if you want. I'm a good listener."

He forced a smile. "Thanks, but it's nothing I want to talk about."

She tugged on his arm, bringing him to a stop, then moved around to stand in front of him. "I really am a good listener." She ran the palm of her hand over his chest, slowly, sensuously. "You must know how I feel, Ethan. I've never made any secret of the fact that…"

He placed his hand over her mouth. "Don't, Millie. Don't say anything you'll regret later."

She licked his palm, then clasped his hand in hers. "Is there someone else?"

He started to say no, and then nodded.

"Is it serious?"

He thought about Cindy, about how wrong he was for her, and how much he wanted her. Was he doing the right thing by letting her go?

"Ethan?"

"No," he said heavily. "It's not serious." Not anymore.

Millie linked her arm through his. "Well, come on, then. I'll fix you a drink at my place and we can watch a movie or something."

"Sure," he said. "Why not?"

Cindy turned on the radio. Sat down in the chair beside the window. Opened the paperback novel she had picked up at the lending library at the lodge, and tried to read. But she didn't see the words on the page. She saw Ethan holding another woman in his arms. Laughing with her. Leaving with her.

With a grimace, she tossed the book across the room.

And then even the radio turned traitor. Was everyone against her? She hadn't heard that song in five years. Their song. Why now? she thought miserably.

Rising, she left her cabin. For a moment, she stood undecided, torn by the desire to go by Ethan's cabin and see if he was there. No! She wouldn't spy on him. Resolutely, she turned in the opposite direction.

She hadn't gone far when she heard his voice, accompanied by feminine laughter. Ducking behind a tree, she saw Ethan and the redheaded woman walking toward the bungalows where the help lived. Cindy didn't miss the way the woman was clinging to Ethan's arm, or the way she was looking up at him, her eyes no doubt filled with adoration!

Cindy stood there, her fingernails digging into the tree trunk, as she watched Ethan follow the woman into one of the bungalows. And close the door.

She stayed there for a long time, silent tears trickling down her cheeks. She could see the woman through the window of the bungalow, doing something in the kitchen. A short time later, all the lights went out in the bungalow.

And all her dreams of the future went out with them.

Chapter Twelve

"You look like the devil."

Cindy stared up at Paul, bleary-eyed. He looked far too cheerful. "You say the sweetest things," she muttered.

He gave her a quick kiss on the cheek. "Rough night?"

"Can we just go and get something to eat? I need a cup of coffee."

"Sure, Cyn."

They walked up to the lodge without saying a word. Paul held the door for her and she headed for the nearest table. It wasn't until she sat down that she saw Ethan sitting at a table across the room. Dressed in a dark red shirt open at the throat, and a pair of faded blue jeans, he looked good enough to eat.

He glanced up just then, his gaze lingering on hers, his expression one of...what? Regret? Relief? Before she could decide, Paul sat down, blocking her view.

She picked up the menu, wondering why she had ever agreed to spend this day with Paul, when all she wanted to do was sit in her cabin and cry.

"Morning, folks, what can I get for you?"

Cindy felt the long green fingers of jealousy twist around her heart when she looked up and saw Millie waiting to take their order.

"What'll you have, Cyn?" Paul asked.

"A strawberry waffle," she said, certain she would never be able to swallow past the lump in her throat. "And coffee."

Paul ordered a poached egg, toast, orange juice and coffee.

Cindy leaned a little to one side so she could watch Millie refill Ethan's coffee cup. She didn't miss the way the waitress smiled at him, or the fact that she touched his shoulder.

"So," Paul said, "I thought maybe we'd go into town today and have a look around. Maybe take in a movie and then go out for dinner. What do you say?"

"Sure, whatever you want to do."

"I need to get back to work." He grinned. "I've left Clarke in charge long enough. He's liable to forget who's the boss. I thought we'd leave tomorrow morning after breakfast. Can you be ready then?"

"I'm not ready to go home."

"Come on, you've played the spoiled little rich girl long enough. It's time to get back to the real world. Your parents are expecting us for brunch tomorrow." He reached across the table and took her hand in his. "We can talk about the wedding then."

"Paul, I'm not going to marry you."

As usual, he wasn't listening to a word she said. "I don't suppose we'd better plan another big wedding, but we can make up for it at the reception."

"Paul!" She slammed her hand on the table. Then, remembering they weren't alone, she lowered her voice. "Would you for once listen to me? It's over. I don't love you. I am not going to marry you. Not now. Not ever."

"I think you mean that."

"I do."

A muscle worked in his jaw. He looked at her as though seeing her, really seeing her, for the first time. Then, very deliberately, he folded his napkin and put it on the table. Rising, he reached into his pocket and withdrew a twenty dollar bill, which he dropped beside his napkin.

"Very well," he said tersely. "Goodbye, Cynthia."

Feeling only relief, she watched him walk out the door. The fact that she wasn't the least bit upset proved all too clearly that she didn't love him, and never had. The only bad thing about his going was that she now had a clear view of Ethan. He met her gaze, one brow arching inquisitively.

Ignoring him, she picked up her cup and sipped her coffee, pretending to be absorbed in the view out the window.

Millie brought their order a few moments later. "Can I bring you anything else?" she asked.

"No, thank you."

To her surprise, Cindy had an appetite, after all. She not only ate her waffle and Paul's egg, but drank his orange juice and his coffee, as well.

When she was finished, she left the dining room, careful to avoid Ethan's gaze.

Outside, she took a deep breath and then headed for the game room, suddenly eager to be in the midst of other people.

Ethan leaned back in his chair, frowning thoughtfully. From the looks of it, Cindy and Mr. Moneybags had had another falling out. A permanent one this time? It would be easy enough to check. Ethan's meals were on the house, but he dropped a few dollars on the table for Millie before he left the dining room.

Dorothea looked up from behind the desk when he entered the office. "Morning, Nephew," she said cheerfully. "Anything wrong?"

"No. Did that greenhorn check out?"

Dorothea lifted one brow. "They're all greenhorns. Which one are you talking about? As if I didn't know," she muttered under her breath.

"Did he?"

"Yes, just a few minutes ago." She grinned at him. "I'd say that leaves the field wide open."

Ethan glared at her.

"Oh, stop looking at me like that," she said. "It's as plain as snow on the mountains that you've got it bad for that girl. Why don't you do something about it before it's too late?"

"It's already too late."

"It's never too late."

Ethan made a low sound of disapproval in his throat. "Her family would never approve of me, and you know it. They think I'm scum."

"Well, change their minds! You're a bright boy. Not bad looking. Are you going to give up, just like that?" she asked, snapping her fingers. "Where's the boy I knew? The one who fought for what he wanted? The one who wanted to be a warrior?"

"I don't know," he muttered. "Where is he?"

"Ethan Stormwalker! Stop talking like that right now, hear? I'm not too old to take you over my knee and whip some sense into you if I have to."

He couldn't help it; he laughed.

"All right, go on with you, now. Aren't you supposed to be giving riding lessons to the Petersen girls in a little while?"

"Yes, ma'am, I'm on my way."

"And watch out for that oldest one. She's got a crush on you, you know."

Ethan grunted, all too aware that Linda Petersen thought she was in love with him. If only Cindy looked at him the way the Petersen girl did! Settling his hat on his head, he left the office. Cindy had looked at him like that once, and if he had anything to do with it, she would again.

Cindy wandered around the game room, but nothing caught her interest. She didn't feel like reading. She wasn't into video games. She had already seen the movie that was playing in the back room. She nodded and smiled at several other guests and then left the building. A swim sounded good, but she didn't have a bathing suit. She was on her way to the gift shop to see if they had one there when she heard Ethan's voice.

She followed it to a small corral behind the barn. Nancy and Mary Petersen were sitting on the top rail of the corral. Inside, Ethan was giving riding lessons to Linda, who was paying more attention to Ethan than to her horse.

Standing out of sight, Cindy watched him interact with the girls. He was patient with Linda, sidestepping her attempts to flirt with him in a way that wouldn't hurt the teenager's feelings, and still managing to teach her how to maintain her seat and hold the reins. He was equally patient with the two younger girls, helping them to gain confidence in themselves and their ability.

Cindy stayed there through the rest of the lesson, happy to watch him, thinking that he would make a wonderful father.

She ducked back when he opened the corral gate for the girls, nodding and smiling as they expressed their thanks for the lesson.

Cindy was about to turn away when she heard Ethan's voice. "You can come out now."

She froze, wondering whether she should run away or

step out from her hiding place and admit she'd been spying on him.

"I know you're there," he said.

Squaring her shoulders, she stepped out from behind the shed and walked toward the corral. "How'd you know I was there?"

"Smelled you."

"Right."

He shrugged. "It's true."

"What do I smell like?"

"Peaches."

She felt a blush climb into her cheeks. She had washed her hair that morning with peach-scented shampoo.

He unsaddled the horse, removed the bridle and turned it loose. "What are you doing here?" He lifted one brow. "You're not signed up for riding lessons, are you?"

"No."

Removing his hat, he ducked between the rails and walked toward her. "Well?"

She looked up at him, the beat of her pulse increasing at his nearness. "Can't we have a truce?"

"I didn't realize we were at war." He held up his hand. "Okay, okay, truce. There's a dance at the lodge tonight after dinner."

"Another one?"

"They have them every Friday and Saturday night. I'll pick you up at eight, if that's all right with you."

"I'll be ready."

Life was certainly uncertain, she mused as she walked back to her cabin. Last week at this time she had been standing at the altar beside Paul, her palms damp, her insides churning. Today, she was smiling inside and out.

She showered, washed her hair and shaved her legs, and all the time her stomach was fluttering in anticipation. She spritzed herself with perfume, then put on her dark blue sundress and regarded herself in the mirror. Not bad. Her hair fell in soft waves around her face. The dress was flattering with its fitted waist and full skirt.

She applied her makeup carefully, sprayed on just a little more perfume, then sat down to wait. A few minutes later, she checked the time, then got up to look out the window. Not wanting Ethan to see her looking for him, she sat down again, crossing and uncrossing her legs. She nearly jumped out of her chair when he knocked on the door.

She counted to five before she answered it. "Hi."

"Hi."

Tall, dark and devastating—that was how he looked. He wore a pair of black jeans, a white shirt and a Western-style leather jacket.

"You ready?" he asked.

She nodded.

"You look good enough to eat," he said, his voice low and husky.

"So do you."

He gazed down at her, his dark eyes moving over her. "I hope you're hungry."

"What?"

He smiled at her, reminding her of the wolf in Little Red Riding Hood. "For dinner," he said smoothly, but they both knew he wasn't talking about food. "And maybe a little dancing. Are you ready to go?"

"Yes, just let me get my sweater." She slipped it over her shoulders, grabbed her bag and put her hand in the hand of the Big Bad Wolf.

There was a different band on the stage tonight.

"Locals from town," Ethan explained. "They alternate between playing here and at one of the clubs in town every other Saturday night. They have quite a following."

"That must be good for business," she said, noting that

the lodge was more crowded than she had ever seen it. She also noticed that there weren't any children, no doubt because more than soft drinks were being served at the bar.

They ordered steak and baked potatoes for dinner and then Ethan gestured at the dance floor. "Shall we?"

She nodded and he led her onto the floor. The band was playing "Cherish," which had always been one of Cindy's favorites. She sighed as Ethan drew her into his arms. It felt so right to be there, to rest her head against his chest, to hear his heart beating sure and strong beneath her ear.

As they glided around the floor, she closed her eyes, oblivious to everyone and everything else but his arms around her, and the faint scent of his aftershave lotion.

They danced the next dance and the next, and when they returned to the table, their dinner was waiting. Caught up in being with Ethan, warmed by the look in his eye, she hardly tasted a bite of her steak.

When they were finished eating, Ethan dropped a few dollars on the table and after getting them both something to drink he took her hand and they went outside.

They walked around the side of the lodge until they found a place where they could be alone. Cindy leaned against the building. She could still hear the music from inside.

"It's a beautiful night," she remarked. "The stars look so close, it seems you could almost reach up and touch one."

"Almost," Ethan agreed.

"Look!" she exclaimed, pointing. "A shooting star! Make a wish, quick."

He laughed softly. "You don't still believe that, do you? It's kid stuff."

"Maybe I'm still a kid."

He drained his glass and set it on the rail of the veranda. "You don't look like a kid."

"Don't I?"

"No." He took the glass from her hand and set it alongside his. "You look like a woman who's waiting to be kissed."

She tilted her head to one side. "Do I?" she whispered.

He nodded as he closed the distance between them. "Am I reading you wrong? Tell me now if I am."

"Just kiss me, Ethan. Just…"

She moaned softly as his mouth covered hers. His arms tightened around her waist, making her heart beat faster. Her blood seemed to slow and thicken in her veins as he deepened the kiss.

She was breathless when he drew back. "Cindy."

"What?"

His hands moved up and down her arms, sending little shivers dancing over her skin. "Can we try again?"

"Oh, Ethan…"

"Is that a yes?"

"Yes!"

"Listen," he said, "they're playing our song."

She moved into his arms again and they danced under the moonlight. It was magical, she thought, the night, the music and Ethan's arms around her.

"Can we go riding in the morning?" she asked as they walked back to her cabin.

"No. I'm going over to the rez tomorrow. They're having a powwow and my uncle is having a sweat."

"You're leaving? How long will you be gone?"

"A day, maybe two. I wouldn't go, but I promised my uncle I'd be there."

"Oh." She couldn't keep the disappointment out of her voice.

"Do you want to come with me?"

"Could I?"

"Sure."

She smiled up at him. "I'd love to. What time are you leaving"

"Seven-thirty."

"In the morning?"

They were at her cabin now. Ethan pulled her into his arms and kissed the tip of her nose. "In the morning. Be ready. Bring a change of clothes, in case we decide to spend the night."

Chapter Thirteen

He was there bright and early the following morning. "You ready, sleepyhead?"

She nodded.

He grinned at her. "Come on," he said, picking up her suitcase, "you can sleep in the truck."

"Sounds good to me." Yawning, she followed him to the pickup and climbed into the passenger seat.

Ethan dropped her suitcase into the bed of the truck alongside his duffel bag, then slid behind the wheel and switched on the ignition. He tugged on her arm. "What are you doing way over there?"

Cindy grinned as she moved closer to him and rested her head on his shoulder.

"How long will it take to get there?"

"Couple of hours. Get some sleep."

She yawned again. "I think I will." Scooting down, she put her head on his thigh and closed her eyes. She was asleep by the time he turned onto the road.

Ethan glanced down at her from time to time, wondering

what she would think when she saw the reservation. It was probably a mistake, bringing her there. Most whites were appalled by what they saw, and with good reason. Still, if he and Cindy were going to have a future together, she needed to see where he came from, and he needed to see her reaction to it.

She sat up as he turned off the highway onto the bumpy dirt road. "Are we there?"

"Just about."

Cindy looked out the window. She wasn't sure what she had expected to see, but this wasn't it. The houses were mostly small, square and in need of paint. There were no lawns, few trees, a scattering of flower beds. There were a lot of rusty old cars and trucks, and here and there an old sofa or chair, the upholstery worn-out and faded by the sun. She saw dogs running in packs. The road had potholes the size of small craters. She remembered getting some literature in the mail about conditions on Indian reservations. The main thing she remembered reading was that Pine Ridge Reservation was located in the poorest county in the United States, that the reservation unemployment rate was 85%, and that 69% of the children lived below the poverty level. Looking around, she could see why this land had been given to the Indians. Who else would want it?

"Your uncle lives here?" she asked.

Ethan nodded. He could tell, by the tone of her voice and the expression on her face, that she was just as appalled by her surroundings as he had expected her to be.

They drove through the heart of the reservation toward a huge clearing where several large tarps and dozens of smaller ones were set up.

Every Lakota on the reservation must be there, Cindy thought. She saw men in breechclouts and moccasins, men in vests and leggings, men in colorful dance costumes and feathers. The women wore cotton blouses and full skirts, or

shirts and jeans, or elegant doeskin dresses elaborately
beaded and fringed. Colorful shawls were draped over their
shoulders.

Long tables laden with Indian arts and crafts were set up
in the shade of the tarps.

Hundreds of tourists milled around, looking at the mer-
chandise, eating hot dogs and hamburgers.

The sound of drumming came from the dance arena.

Ethan parked the truck, got out, came around and opened
the door for her. "I'm not dancing until later," he said. "Do
you want to walk around for a while?"

"Sure."

They wandered up and down the aisles, looking at the
different things for sale. Cindy admired the paintings, some
done on canvas, others drawn on deer hide, some done on
rocks and wood. There were numerous rattles made out of
gourds or turtle shells, and ceremonial masks adorned with
feathers. There were buckskin shirts and colorful calico
dresses, T-shirts painted with Indians or horses or buffalo,
vests and scarves, feathered war bonnets and beaded moccasins. One table held spears and war clubs, as well as
knives of all sizes, the handles made of wood or bone or
metal. Several booths sold audiocassettes of Lakota music,
as well as flutes and drums in assorted shapes and sizes.
There were pretty Native American dolls, brightly beaded
chokers, woven baskets, a wide assortment of jewelry
crafted in silver and turquoise, fetishes carved in onyx. And
every table seemed to offer dream catchers in a wide variety
of sizes and colors.

She picked up a small blue-and-white one. "It's pretty,
isn't it?"

Ethan nodded. "My people believe that long ago, when
the world was young, one of their elders sat atop a high
mountain, seeking wisdom. As he sat there, Iktomi appeared
to him in the form of a spider. While they spoke, Iktomi

took the elder's hoop, which was decorated with feathers, beads and horse hair, and began to spin a web. And as he worked, he spoke to the elder about the cycles of life—infant to child, child to adult, adult to elder, when one must be cared for as an infant. There were many forces in life, Iktomi said, some good, some bad.

"And all the while he spoke, Iktomi continued to weave his web, starting from the outside and working inward. 'You see,' the spider said as he returned the hoop to the elder, 'the web is a circle but there is a hole in the center. If you believe in the Great Spirit, the web will catch your good ideas and dreams, but the bad ones will go through the hole and be lost.' So it is that dream catchers are hung above the beds of my people to sift their dreams and visions. The good things are captured in the web of life, but the bad things escape through the hole in the web and are no longer a part of them."

"What a wonderful story."

Ethan nodded at the dream catcher in her hand. "Do you want it?"

"Yes."

He paid for it, and the man behind the table placed it in a small brown paper sack, which he handed to Cindy.

"Thank you," she said, and kissed Ethan on the cheek.

She tucked the paper sack into her handbag as they made their way toward the dance area. Taking her by the hand, Ethan led her around the inside edge of the arena. There were several rows of benches, most of them occupied. Some had blankets draped over them to reserve a space. Ethan led her to a bench covered with a red blanket. There were two lawn chairs behind the bench. Ethan sat down in one of the chairs.

"Should we sit here?" she asked, sitting in the chair beside his.

"Sure. The red blanket is for me. My uncle put it there. The benches are for dancers only."

"Oh."

Cindy glanced around. The head drum was placed under an arbor supported by four upright posts and covered with branches and leaves to protect the drum from the sun.

A dozen women were performing the Fancy Shawl Dance, their bodies moving in graceful rhythm to the beat of the drum. They were bending this way and that, their steps so quick and light that they looked as though they were literally dancing on air. They wore ankle-high moccasins and leggings, flared skirts, and blouses with beaded yokes. Colorful belts enhanced their waists. But it was their shawls that held the eye—beautiful shawls with long fringe.

The men's fancy dance was next. Ethan told her the fancy dance had started in Oklahoma and had spread all over the country. The dancers wore roaches and colorful bustles and beaded headbands. Their steps were almost too fast to follow.

The next dancer was a handsome teenage boy who performed the hoop dance. Clad in only a breechclout and moccasins, he twirled and bent and twisted in ways that looked impossible, his body moving fluidly as he passed the hoops over his body—first two hoops, then four, then six, then eight, each movement producing a different effect, each one more complex than the last.

Cindy applauded with the rest of the crowd, and then it was time for Ethan to go and get ready.

"Will you be all right here?" he asked.

She assured him that she would, though she felt a little out of place sitting there surrounded by people she didn't know. She didn't miss the speculative looks cast in her direction as Ethan walked away.

She gazed around the arena, noting that there were several flags flying at one side of the emcee's table. The U.S. flag was there, and a military flag. There was also an eagle staff, which was about six feet high, with eagle feathers attached to it. Ethan had told her once that the eagle staff served as the tribal flag.

A short time later, the emcee announced the next dance, which was the Men's Traditional Dance. Ethan had told her that the Lakota were credited with the origination of this dance and that, years ago, only a few warriors were entitled to wear the roach and bustle of the traditional dance. The Lakota style of the dance was called Northern Traditional.

A dozen men filed into the arena. In spite of the feathers and paint he wore, Cindy spotted Ethan immediately. The costumes were elaborate and colorful, with fancy head-dresses, breastplates, bandoliers, angora anklets and moccasins, as well as fringed arm bands and cuffs. Some of the dancers carried a large wing fan, others a dance staff.

But Cindy had eyes only for Ethan, his steps and movements that of a warrior searching for prey. She had always been fascinated by his Native American heritage and beliefs, never more so than now, when he looked both alien and familiar.

The rest of the day passed in a blur of color and motion underscored by the constant beat of the drum. She met Ethan's uncle, Larry Two Hawks, a tall spare man with a sharp nose and twinkling eyes. She met Ethan's friends, some of whom he had known since childhood; she met his cousins, an aunt, his grandmother. They all smiled and made her feel welcome, though she could see the curiosity in their eyes.

Late that night, she and Ethan found a place to be alone.

"So," he said, keeping his voice carefully neutral so she wouldn't know how important her answer was, "what do you think?"

"I love it!" she said enthusiastically. "All of it. And your family, they're so nice, although a few of them looked at me kind of funny."

He drew her into his arms. "Probably because I've never brought a woman home before."

She didn't miss the significance of those few words. "Do you have a house here?" The thought made her shudder inwardly. Were the insides of the houses as dreary as the outsides?

"No. My mother has a house here but it's closed up. I usually stay over at my uncle's place."

"Is your mother here today?" Cindy asked, wondering why she hadn't met her.

"No, she lives in Bozeman now. I'll take you to meet her one of these days. She never comes to the rez anymore."

"Why not?"

"I don't know. I think she had a falling out with her brother years ago, but I'm not sure. I asked her about it once, but she refused to talk about it." His gaze lingered on her lips. "And I don't want to talk about it, either," he said, his voice husky.

And lowering his head, he kissed her.

Just a simple kiss, yet it made her chest tighten and played havoc with her breathing. She leaned into him, wanting more, and he willingly obliged, his mouth covering hers, his tongue a fiery dart that threatened to burn her up from the inside out.

Feeling suddenly weak in the knees, she wrapped her arms around him.

He smiled down at her, all too aware of the effect his kisses were having on her.

"It's late," he said. "We'd better turn in."

"Where will we stay tonight?"

"I think we'd better go to my uncle's," Ethan said.

"Oh?" She couldn't keep the disappointment out of her voice.

He nodded. "I don't trust myself to be alone with you. Not tonight."

It was the right thing, the smart thing, so why didn't she feel happier about it?

The next day passed all too quickly. Cindy loved watching the dancing—the costumes, the music, the excitement. She didn't think she would ever get tired of it.

She and Ethan made small talk on the way home. He had been prepared for her to be somewhat critical of reservation life. Knowing where she lived and how she had been brought up, he had thought she might look down her nose at his people and the way they lived, but she never expressed anything except admiration for his people, and he loved her all the more because of it.

"I overheard your uncle telling some of the kids a story," she said, "but I didn't hear the end."

"What story?"

"Something about an eagle and a prairie chicken."

Ethan nodded. "I remember that one. He told it to me when I was young."

She nudged him in the side with her elbow. "Well, tell me!"

He looked thoughtful for a moment. "The way I recall it, there was a brave who found an eagle's egg and placed it in a prairie chicken's nest. The eagle hatched with the prairie chicken's young and grew up with them.

"Thinking he was a prairie chicken, the eagle spent his life doing what the chickens did. He scratched in the dirt for seeds and ate insects. He clucked and he cackled. And when he flew, it was with a great thrashing of wings, and then only for a short distance a short way off the ground, because that was the way the prairie chickens flew.

"Years passed, and the eagle grew old. One day he saw a beautiful bird soaring high above him. The bird floated with graceful majesty on the powerful wind currents, soaring with scarcely a beat of its strong golden wings.

"'What a beautiful bird!' the eagle said to his neighbor. 'What is it?'

"'That's an eagle,' his neighbor said, 'the chief of all the birds. But don't give him a second thought. You could never be like him.'

"So the changeling eagle never gave it a second thought and died thinking he was a prairie chicken. Built to soar high in the heavens, but conditioned to stay earthbound, it lived its whole life pecking at seeds and eating insects and never reached the heights for which it had been born."

"That's a wonderful story!" Cindy said, and then she looked at him and grinned. "Reminds me of that bumper sticker from a few years ago that said Don't Let the Turkeys Get You Down."

"Yeah. My uncle always told me I could be anything I wanted to be, as long as I believed it."

"What do you want to be?"

Ethan slid a quick glance in her direction. "Just what I am."

"You're happy working for your aunt on the ranch? You don't want to be a doctor or a lawyer?"

"Not even an Indian chief," he said with a grin. "I'm happy just being one of the Indians."

"But you could be so much more."

"One day the ranch will be mine. My aunt has no one else to leave it to. I'll never be rich, but I'm happy there. I like the life, I like being my own boss. I like being close to the rez."

Cindy nodded, but didn't say anything.

Ethan blew out a sigh. She loved him. He didn't doubt that for a minute. And he loved her, but maybe love wasn't enough when two people were as different as they were.

"I forgot to tell you," he said. "I'm taking a group out on an overnight ride tomorrow."

"Oh?"

"Yeah, they want to rough it. You know, camp out, cook over an open fire, sleep under the stars."

"Sounds awful," she said. "Can I go?"

"I wish you could."

"Why can't I?"

"All the horses are spoken for except one, and he's lame."

"Oh."

"It's only one night."

"I know, but we've missed so many already."

They pulled into the ranch yard a few minutes later. Ethan parked the car in front of her cabin and drew her into his arms.

She looked up at him. "Don't you want to come in?"

"We're leaving at six tomorrow morning." He kissed the tip of her nose. "And I've got a lot to do before then."

"All right."

He ran his finger down her cheek, then tapped it against her lips. "Try to miss me a little, okay?"

"Maybe."

"Maybe?" He pulled her against him and kissed her, his hands caressing her back, delving into her hair.

"Okay, okay," she said with a teasing grin. "I'll miss you."

"That's better...."

"A little," she said.

He gave a low growl deep in his throat, then kissed her again, until her insides felt like they were melting.

"Okay," she said breathlessly. "A lot."

"I'll see you as soon as I get back."

"All right. Be careful. Ethan?"

"What?"

"One more kiss?"

He obliged her gladly, his kiss a brand and a promise.

She climbed out of the truck reluctantly, and stood there staring after him as he drove away, her heart filled to the brim. He did love her. Even though he hadn't said the words, she knew it was true.

Chapter Fourteen

A steady pounding on the door roused her some time later. She woke reluctantly, not wanting to leave her dream behind and face reality. It had been such a lovely dream. She had been sitting with Ethan beside a quiet stream that meandered through a sunlit meadow. He had been leaning forward, his dark eyes alight with desire, focused on her lips....

Throwing the covers aside, she reached for her robe and padded barefoot to the door. She opened it, yawning.

"You still in bed?"

"Ethan! What are you doing here? Do you know what time it is?"

"A quarter after seven," he said, sweeping her into his arms. "I should be at the stable. Instead, there are twelve guests cooling their heels while I stand here, waiting for a kiss."

"Better take more than one, then," she said, smiling up at him, "to make their wait worthwhile."

He kissed her and kissed her again. "Remember, you promised to miss me," he said.

"I remember. I miss you already."

"With you here, waiting for me, they may not get as long a trip as they want." He claimed her lips once more in a fiercely possessive kiss, gave her a hug that nearly cracked her ribs, and was gone.

She was still smiling when she climbed back into bed and fell asleep, only to be awakened a short time later by the ringing of the phone.

She answered on the fourth ring. "Hello?"

"Cynthia?"

She sat up. "Mom?"

"You've got to come home right away! Your father…"

"What is it? What's wrong?"

"He's in the hospital… His heart…it's bad, honey."

"I'll rent a car and be home as soon as I can. Try not to worry."

"Hurry."

"I will. I love you, Mom. See you soon."

She hung up the phone and scrambled out of bed. Twenty minutes later, she was dressed and packed and waiting for someone to drive her into town. Her dad was in the hospital. Cindy could barely grasp it. He had always been so strong, so indomitable. As a little girl, she had idolized him, and like all little girls, she had planned to marry him when she grew up. He had always been there for her, comforting her when her best friend had moved to Rhode Island, going trick or treating with her on Halloween. He had taken her side when her biology teacher had accused her of cheating on a test, had missed several weekends on the golf course to stay home and teach her to shoot baskets so she could beat her brother at one-on-one. When she wanted a canopy bed, he had bought it for her. Cindy wished she had told him she loved him the last time she'd talked to him on the phone. What if she never got another chance?

It wasn't until she was in the truck headed down the highway that she realized she had forgotten to leave a note for Ethan.

It was late afternoon when she reached home. She left the car in the driveway and ran up the stairs and into the house.

"Mom?"

"She's not here."

Cindy whirled around to see Reyna, the housekeeper, standing in the kitchen doorway. "Where is she? My dad..."

"She's at the hospital. He took a turn for the worse early this morning. The doctor—"

Cindy didn't wait to hear more. Grabbing her handbag and the car keys, she ran back outside.

The traffic was heavy at this time of day, adding to the tension that was drawing her nerves tighter with every passing minute. She drove with both hands on the wheel, all her attention focused on the road ahead of her. She couldn't think of her dad, not now, or she'd burst into tears.

She pulled into the hospital parking lot ten minutes later and parked the car, then sat there staring at the building. She hated hospitals—the look of them, the antiseptic smell, the sickly green walls.

Taking a deep breath, she got out of the car and hurried across the parking lot and into the lobby.

A receptionist sat behind a curved desk. She looked up at the sound of Cindy's footsteps. "May I help you?" she asked.

"Could you please tell me what room Jordan Wagner is in?"

The receptionist looked through a card file. "He's on the third floor in Intensive Care."

"Thank you."

Cindy didn't have to ring for an elevator; one was waiting. She stepped inside and pushed 3, then clenched her hands together as the car rose upward. Moments later, she stepped out into a wide hallway. She followed the arrows to ICU and found her mother sitting on a chair outside the double doors.

"Mom?"

"Cynthia!" Her mother rose and hurried toward her.

Cindy threw her arms around her and hugged her close. "How is he?"

"He's bad. They'll only let me in for five minutes every hour."

"Are you holding up okay? Have you called Uncle Jimmy? Come on, let's sit down."

Cindy led her mother back to the row of chairs that lined the wall and they sat side by side, holding hands. Her mother looked worn-out. There were dark shadows under her eyes, and her hair was slightly mussed.

"Jimmy and Ilsa will be here tonight."

"What happened? Daddy's never been sick a day in his life."

Tears dripped down her mother's cheeks. "We were watching the *Late Show*. Your father got up to get us something to drink…." She shook her head. "I heard a noise in the kitchen, and when I went in there, he was on the floor. He hit his head on the edge of the counter. He's got a nasty cut on the back of his head."

"Why didn't you call me when it happened?"

"I tried, but the line was busy every time I called and then things got hectic and…" Claire took a deep shuddering breath. "I was so upset, the doctor gave me a sedative and it knocked me out."

"It's all right, Mom, I'm here now."

"The doctor said his heart's probably been bad for a long time. He said he's surprised it hadn't happened before now. You know your dad. He never goes in for a checkup like he should, never takes a day off. And he refused to stop smoking, even though I begged him to." She squeezed Cindy's hands. "I'm so afraid."

"I know, Mom, but he'll be okay. He has to be." Cindy forced a smile. "He's too ornery to die."

Claire sniffed and smiled through her tears. "I'm so glad you're here. Did you have a good time at the ranch?"

Cindy nodded. "He was there, Mom."

"Paul? Yes, I know. He called. He'll be here tomorrow."

"No, not Paul. Ethan."

"That Indian dancer? He was at the dude ranch? Is that why you went there?"

"No. His aunt owns it. I didn't know he was going to be there."

"Is he the reason you left Paul?"

"I still love Ethan, Mom, more than ever."

"Cynthia, honey…"

"Don't say it."

"Well, whatever you do, don't mention it to your father. Not now!"

"Where's Lance?"

"He went on vacation with the Longs. They're back-packing in the mountains. There's no way to reach them."

"And Joe?" Her older brother was a lawyer in Boston.

"He'll be here as soon as he can."

It was a long day. They took turns going in to see her father. Cindy was shocked at how old and thin he looked. His skin was pale and cool, his cheeks sunken. He was surrounded by monitors, with wires and tubes going every-where. It was a frightening thing to see.

She and her mother went down to the cafeteria for dinner, though neither of them had much of an appetite.

Cindy tried to make small talk, hoping to take their minds off the seriousness of her father's condition, but she quickly ran out of things to say. Nothing else seemed important, not with her father so close to death.

Her mother went in to see him when they went back upstairs. Cindy sat on one of the hard chairs and thought about Ethan. He'd be stretched out in his bedroll now, out under the stars. Was he thinking about her? Did they really have a chance to patch things up between them? Their backgrounds were so different, yet what did that really matter if they loved each other? He was a smart man. He wouldn't have any trouble finding a job here in town. They could get an apartment close to her folks. And she could work, too. She frowned. There was always a chance that Ethan might want to stay on at the ranch. That would take some getting used to, but she was willing to give it a try, if that was what he wanted. Sooner or later, their families would just have to accept them, and if not... She didn't want to think about that. She loved her parents, and she knew Ethan had a great love and respect for his mother. Somehow, they would make it work!

Ethan folded his arms behind his head and gazed up at the stars wheeling across the sky. It had been a good ride and now everyone was settled down for the night. He could hear one of the men snoring nearby. An owl hooted in the distance. A horse stamped its foot.

It was a beautiful night, warm and clear. If Cindy had been there beside him, it would have been perfect. He could hardly believe she was back in his life. Was he making a mistake, thinking they could pick up where they'd left off? Nothing had really changed. She was still a spoiled rich girl, and he was still an Indian with a police record.

He shook his head, remembering the night he had been arrested. It had been shortly after their breakup. He had been in a bar, drinking with a couple of buddies, their girlfriends and a pretty blonde they were trying to set him up with. He rarely had more than a beer or two, but that night he was downing whiskey shooters in an effort to forget a raven-haired girl with sky-blue eyes. He was well and truly drunk when some dude wearing a ten-gallon hat, a cowhide vest and matching boots started making cracks about Indians dating white women. Ethan had held his temper as long as possible, but he'd lost it when the *wasichu* started hitting on his date. Ethan had told the man to back off. The man had made a suggestion that was not only crude but physically impossible. The hot words between them had soon turned to blows, and the next thing Ethan knew, he was behind bars for being drunk and disorderly. Dorothea had come to his rescue. He didn't think he would ever get over the humiliation he'd felt when he found himself behind bars. Even now, the memory filled him with shame and remorse, made him feel he wasn't good enough for Cindy, even though he'd rarely had a drink since that night.

He grinned faintly as he saw a shooting star streak across the sky. Cindy always closed her eyes and made a wish on a shooting star. He had often teased her about it, but tonight he closed his eyes and made a wish of his own.

Chapter Fifteen

Rudy rode up alongside Ethan. "Where are you going? The Creek Trail is that way."

"We're taking a short cut."

"Short cut?" Rudy glanced at his watch. "We'll be back at the ranch three hours early if we go this way."

Ethan nodded. The ride was supposed to last until dusk, but he couldn't wait that long to see Cindy again.

"Some of the guests are liable to complain," Rudy remarked.

"I doubt it." Ethan glanced over his shoulder to where the riders were strung out behind him. Most of them looked more than ready to call it a day.

"You're the boss," Rudy said.

Ethan grunted softly and urged Dakota into a canter.

"Gone?" Damn, he never should have taken her to the reservation, never let her see where he'd come from. "What do you mean, she's gone?"

Dorothea shook her head. "Calm down, Nephew."

"Where did she go?"

"How should I know?" his aunt asked wryly. "Tourists rarely leave a forwarding address."

Ethan swore under his breath. He'd spent the last two days thinking of her here, waiting for him. He'd been counting the hours until he could see her again, and she hadn't even been here.

"I'll see you later," he said.

Dorothea waved at him, then turned to answer the phone.

His hand was on the screen door when his aunt called his name. He glanced over his shoulder to see her holding the phone out toward him. "It's her," she said, as he approached the counter.

He took a deep breath as he reached for the phone. "Hello?"

"Ethan, hi."

"Hi yourself."

"Are you all right?" she asked. "You sound kind of funny."

"Do I? Maybe that's because I expected you to be here when I got back." He laughed bitterly. "You're making quite a habit of running away."

"Is that what you think I did?"

"Didn't you?" He heard the sneer in his voice and hated himself for it.

"No."

"So you didn't run off? Funny, I don't see you here."

"Ethan, if you'd just listen…"

He reined in his temper as best he could. "Go on, I'm listening."

"My dad had a heart attack."

Ethan swore under his breath.

"I know I should have left you a note, but I didn't think about it until I was on the way home, and then it was too late. This is the first chance I've had to call."

"Cindy, honey, I'm sorry. Is he…"

"It's bad, that's all I know. The doctors haven't said too much, but they don't seem very optimistic."

He heard the tears in her voice, wished he had the right to be there with her, to hold her hand and offer what little support he could. Damn his quick temper and his big mouth. She needed comfort, not a tongue-lashing. "Cindy, listen, I—"

"My mom's calling me. I've got to go. Goodbye, Ethan."

He stared at the phone after she hung up, feeling like a first-class jerk.

"Everything all right?" Dorothea asked.

"No," he muttered, realizing that if he didn't get Cindy back, his life would never be all right again. "I need some time off."

"How much time? We're booked solid through October, and we're short-handed as it is. You know that. I can't spare you right now."

"Dammit!" Ethan brought his fist down on top of the counter.

"Do you want to tell me what this is all about?"

"Cindy's dad had a heart attack. He's in the hospital."

"Did she ask for you to be there?"

"No." He grunted softly. "She called to tell me what had happened, but did I give her a chance to explain? No! I accused her of running off, as if that matters when her old man's at death's door."

"Take the truck," Dorothea said. "It's more reliable than that old car of mine."

"What about…?"

She made a dismissive gesture with her hand. "Don't worry, we'll get by. I can ride drag on the trail rides if I have to. I'll call Two Hawks and ask him to send over some dancers from the rez to fill in for you. Just don't be gone too long."

Leaning over the counter, he planted a kiss on her cheek. "Thanks, Dory," he said, calling her by the nickname he hadn't used since he was a little boy. "Ask Rudy to look after my horse, will ya? Wolf can take care of himself."

"Will do." Reaching under the counter, she plucked the truck keys off a hook and tossed them to him.

He caught them in midair. "I'll make this up to you," he promised.

"Sure you will. Try not to burn up the road between here and there."

Cindy blinked back her tears as she went back to sit with her family. Joe had shown up a short time ago, along with his wife, Kim, and their three kids. Uncle Jimmy and Aunt Ilsa had arrived shortly thereafter. Her father's business partner, Thad Norwood, was also there, apparently having just arrived. They sat in a group, making small talk, drinking Cokes, or coffee from foam cups. Joe's youngest son, Joe, Jr., was asleep on his father's lap.

Cindy shook hands with Mr. Norwood, then sat down beside her mother, wishing Ethan was with her. She was afraid in a way she never had been before, and she wanted him there to keep her fears at bay, to assure her that everything would be all right. And if it wasn't…then she wanted a strong shoulder to cry on. But he wasn't here, and after the way he'd acted on the phone, she had changed her mind about asking if he could possibly come and stay for a day or two.

She blinked back her tears and forced herself to pay attention to what was being said. She couldn't fall apart, not now, not when her mother needed her to be strong. But she didn't feel strong. Just sad and scared and lonely.

At midnight, Joe took his family to the house so Kim could put the kids to bed. Mr. Norwood took his leave about the same time, saying he would call in the morning. Jimmy and Ilsa decided to take a walk and see if they could find something to eat that didn't come out of a vending machine. Her mother was dozing in her chair.

Rising, Cindy stretched the kinks out of her back and shoulders, then picked up her mother's coat and covered her with it. She hated hospitals, hated waiting, hated not knowing if her dad would ever leave this place alive.

Walking down the hall, she stared out the window into the empty darkness, then lowered her head and tried to pray.

She didn't know how long she had stood there when she realized she wasn't alone. Lifting her head, she saw her reflection in the dark glass, and a tall, broad-shouldered man standing behind her. Her heart skipped a beat as she slowly turned to face him.

"Ethan." His name slipped past her lips. He was wearing a white T-shirt, jeans, a cowboy hat and moccasins. She had never been so happy to see anyone in her life.

She went to him without hesitation, closed her eyes as his arms wrapped around her. One prayer, at least, had been answered.

Chapter Sixteen

Ethan held her tight, afraid he might never find the strength to let her go. He could count the times he had been afraid, really gut-wrenchingly scared, on the fingers of one hand, but none of those measured up to the apprehension he had felt while waiting for Cindy to turn around. If she had ignored him, slapped him, told him to get out of her sight and never return, he wouldn't have blamed her. Hell, it would have been no more than he deserved.

He stroked her back, buried his face in the wealth of her hair and held on for dear life. He felt her trembling, felt her tears soaking through his shirt, and held her tighter.

"It's all right," he murmured. "It will be all right. Shh, darlin', don't cry."

Sniffling, she lifted her head to look at him. "I can't believe you're here."

He went suddenly still. "Do you want me to go?"

"No!" She clutched at his shirt. "Don't go. Oh, Ethan, I'm so afraid he's going to die. And he can't die. He just can't!" A great shuddering sob wracked her body. "Our last words to each other were spoken in anger."

He didn't know what to say to that. Instead, he drew her back into his arms and held her close when she began to cry again.

It was then that Claire Wagner woke up. A moment later Joe stepped out of the elevator and Jimmy and Ilsa rounded a corner, carrying a tray filled with sandwiches and cups of coffee.

Cindy didn't know how long she might have stood there, clinging to Ethan, if he hadn't cleared his throat and loosened his hold on her.

Her mother was staring at Ethan as if she was seeing a ghost.

Joe, Jimmy and Ilsa all came to an abrupt halt at the sight of Cindy locked in a stranger's embrace.

If she hadn't been so worried about her father, she would have laughed at the expressions on their faces. Her mother appeared shocked. Joe looked as if he might take a swing at the man who dared hold his sister so intimately. Jimmy seemed faintly puzzled and Ilsa looked envious.

And then, just when Cindy didn't think things could get more awkward, the elevator opened and Paul walked out, looking as if he had just stepped off the cover of *GQ*.

Claire spoke first. Shrugging the coat off her shoulders, she stood up. "Cindy, why don't you introduce your friend."

"Yes, Cindy, why don't you do that?" Paul said, sneering. "I'm sure they'd all like to meet the man you left me for."

Ethan's eyes narrowed ominously.

Cindy squeezed Ethan's arm. "This is Ethan Stormwalker. Ethan, you know my mother, Claire. That's my older brother, Joe, and my aunt and uncle, Ilsa and Jimmy."

Ethan nodded.

"What's he doing here?" Paul asked.

"I could ask the same of you," Ethan retorted.

"Gentlemen, please." Claire moved to stand between the two men. "This isn't the time or the place."

Paul put his arm around Claire's shoulders. "You're right, of course," he said. "I'm sorry."

With the ease in tension, they went to sit down. Paul sat on one side of Claire, Joe sat on the other. Cindy sat next to Ethan, clinging to his hand as if she would never let him go. Jimmy and Ilsa passed out the sandwiches and coffee, and then they, too, sat down.

It was near dawn when the doctor appeared. Cindy squeezed Ethan's hand.

The doctor's gaze moved over each of them, then settled on Claire. "I think he's out of the woods. We'll know for sure by tomorrow night."

Claire sagged against her son, her eyes brimming with tears of relief.

The doctor smiled, obviously pleased to be able to give them good news. "Why don't you all go home and get a good night's sleep? If there's any change one way or another, we'll give you a call."

Claire shook her head. "I don't think—"

Cindy stepped forward and took her mother's hand. "Come on, Mom. He's right. We could all use a good night's rest." She patted her mother's arm. "You don't want Daddy to see you looking like this. He'll wonder why you aren't in the bed beside him."

Her mother laughed softly. "All right." She stood and extended her hand to the doctor. "Thank you. But you will call if there's any change? Any change at all?"

"Certainly. Go home and try not to worry. I'm sure the worst is over."

Cindy helped her mother gather up her things, while Joe rang for the elevator.

Ethan hung back, all too aware that he was not there at Cindy's invitation, and not part of her family.

He stood beside her in the elevator going down, equally aware of her ex-fiancé's doleful expression.

Outside, they all paused under a streetlight.

"Our car's in a lot on the next block," her uncle said. "We'll meet you at the house."

Claire nodded, then turned to Paul. "Thank you for coming. We'll call you if there's any change." It was a clear dismissal.

Paul mumbled something and gave Claire a hug. He glanced at Cindy, who was standing beside Ethan, then looked at Ethan for a long moment, his expression positively lethal, before he walked away.

"Mom, why don't you leave your car here and I'll drive you and Cindy home?" Joe suggested.

"That's a good idea, Mom. I think you should go with Joe," Cindy said. "I think I'll leave my car here, too. That way, I can go with Ethan."

"Wait a minute, Cindy, I don't think you—"

She gave her brother a quelling glance. "It doesn't matter what you think, brother dear," she said, her tone sugary sweet. "I think it's a good idea." She took Ethan by the hand. "Shall we?"

With a nod, he led her to where he'd left the truck. Unlocking the door, he helped her in, then went around to the driver's side and slid behind the wheel. To save his soul, he couldn't think of a thing to say.

She solved the problem for him. "Thank you for coming. You'll never know how much I wanted you here."

"Honey, I'm so sorry for the way I reacted when you called. I had no right to talk to you that way. I should have known you wouldn't leave like that without a good reason. On the drive here…" He grinned ruefully. "I didn't know if you'd even talk to me."

"But you came anyway."

"You were hurting. I didn't know if I could help, but I had to try."

With a wordless cry, she fell into his arms and buried her face against his chest. He held her close and for that moment, he was sure that, in spite of all their differences, they could work it out.

He sat there, content to hold her, until the lights of a hospital security truck flashed across the windshield.

"We'd better go," he said. "The doctor was right. You need to get some sleep."

She cuddled close to his side as he drove her home.

When he turned down her street, he was reminded once again just how vast the gulf between her lifestyle and his really was. There were only a few houses on the block, and they all sat on well-manicured lawns behind wrought-iron gates or high brick walls. There were no potholes in the street, no dogs rummaging through the trash, no rusty cars or old sofas left to rot in the sun, no drunks puking on the side of the road. Ethan swore under his breath. He didn't belong here. Would never belong here.

He pulled up to the gate in front of her house, waited while she rolled down the window and spoke to the guard. Moments later, Ethan pulled through the gate. The driveway was lit by small lanterns all the way up to the front of the house, where a porch light burned brightly. The rest of the house was dark, save for a single lamp in the front window.

Ethan switched off the lights and the engine. "Will I see you tomorrow?"

"Of course." She smothered a yawn behind her hand. "Let's go in. I'm exhausted."

He stared at her, wondering if he'd heard her right. "What?"

"Come on." She tugged on his hand.

"I don't think that's a good idea."

"Well, I do. Come on, you might as well spend the night here instead of looking for a motel."

"I don't think your mother…"

"She won't mind."

"Your brother will."

"Too bad. I live here. He doesn't." She tugged on his hand again, harder this time. "Come on, I'm too tired to argue about this."

Reluctantly, he grabbed his duffel bag out of the back of the truck and followed her up the wide front steps. She opened an elegant door of frosted glass and carved oak, and he followed her through a large foyer with a floor of black and white marble tile, into a large, high-ceilinged room with furniture so pristine and elegant he wondered if it had ever been used.

"The guest rooms are upstairs," she said in a low voice. "Come on."

He followed her up a winding stairway. Thick, forest-green carpet muffled his footsteps.

She stopped in front of a door at the end of the hall. "I hope you'll be comfortable here. Just make yourself at home. There are clean sheets on the bed. It you want to take a shower, there are clean towels in the bathroom." She pointed at the door across the hall. "That's my room."

He stood there, feeling like a green kid with his first date, wondering if he dared kiss her good-night here, in this house.

"Good night, Ethan," she whispered.

"'Night."

Rising on her tiptoes, she slipped one hand behind his neck and kissed him. "Thanks again for coming. I'll see you in the morning."

He nodded, watching the sway of her hips as she crossed the hallway and opened the door to her room. She wore a pair of stretchy black pants that fit like a coat of paint and made his mouth water.

She stepped inside, smiled at him over her shoulder and then closed the door.

Stifling the urge to follow her, he turned and stepped into a room that would have held his mother's whole house.

He dropped his duffel bag on the floor beside the bed and tossed his hat on the back of one of the wooden chairs. "Unbelievable," he muttered as his gaze moved over the room.

The walls were a rich beige color, the carpet a dark chocolate brown, the spread on the king-size bed some sort of brown, blue and white print. There was a curved sofa and a rocking chair covered in the same material. A small round table and two wooden chairs occupied one corner; an antique writing desk stood against one wall. There was a fancy looking lamp on the bedside table. The door beside the bed led into a walk-in closet; the door across from the bed led to a bathroom with a double shower and a sunken bathtub.

He stared at the tub. She'd told him to make himself at home, and while he had never had a home like this one and wasn't likely to ever have one, he decided to take her at her word. Bending over, he turned on the tap.

Cindy had changed into her nightgown and was turning down the covers on her bed when she heard the water running. She glanced over her shoulder, her imagination springing to life at the thought of Ethan taking a bath just across the hall. She wished she had the right to join him in the tub, to wash his back, to share his bed....

She jerked her thoughts away. It wasn't safe to travel that road, or to get her hopes up too high, and yet she couldn't help it. He had left the ranch to come after her. She still couldn't believe it, or forget the way her heart had leaped at the mere sight of him. Nor had she realized how much she needed him until she saw him standing there, tall and strong. No other arms could have comforted her the way his did. And now he was here, in her house. Did he remember the first time he had been here? He had been uncomfortable then. How did he feel now? Could he get past the differences between them? Would seeing where and how she lived drive him away? She had a sudden, vivid image of the reservation. What if he asked her to marry him and live with him there? Could she do it?

She glanced around her room. It was done in shades of blue and green and white. She had a soft bed, warm blankets. Her curtains and bedspread matched the wallpaper. There was a thick carpet on the floor. She had heat in winter and air-conditioning in summer. She had thirty pairs of shoes, two closets filled with clothes and a new car every year. She had a maid to wait on her, a cook who fulfilled her every culinary wish, and parents who loved her. Could she give it all up for Ethan?

In a heartbeat, she thought, and slipping under the covers, she closed her eyes and let her imagination run wild as she pictured Ethan in the tub, just across the hall.

Chapter Seventeen

Ethan woke at first light. Lying there, with his arms folded behind his head, he found his first thought was for Cindy. He spent a pleasant few minutes picturing her curled up under the covers, her tousled hair spread over her pillow like black silk, her skin warm and sleep-scented. He let himself contemplate what it would be like to slip into her room and wrap his nakedness around her, to ease his desire in her sweet flesh. Would she welcome him? Or shout the house down? When the heaviness in his groin became more than he could bear, he thrust her image from his mind and rolled out of bed.

He dressed quickly in a pair of clean jeans and a red plaid shirt, brushed his teeth, combed his hair. For a time, he paced the floor, wondering how much longer it would be until Cindy and her family got up. He didn't feel welcome or comfortable in her house. If he had, he would have gone downstairs and made himself a cup of coffee, but he didn't think that was a good idea. He didn't want her mother accusing him of overstepping his bounds, didn't want to have to explain himself to her brother.

Feeling like a prisoner, he went to stare out the window. From his vantage point he could see a tennis court, a large swimming pool with a Jacuzzi and a waterfall, a lawn that looked like green velvet, a well-tended flower garden, several fruit trees and a gazebo.

Turning away from the window, he muttered, "You're in way over your head here, Stormwalker."

"Why do you say that?"

Damn, he thought, he was losing his edge if a white woman could sneak up on him. Dressed in a dark pink sweater and a pair of white pants, she looked as fresh as a prairie flower. Her hair fell loose over her shoulders, just the way he liked it.

She cocked her head to one side, regarding him through guileless eyes. "Well?"

"I don't belong here."

"That again." In the past, it had been a constant argument between them, his stubborn belief that the differences in their backgrounds and religion would forever keep them apart.

He shook his head, a wry smile lifting one corner of his mouth. "You just don't see it, do you?"

She closed the distance between them and slipped her arms around his neck. "Haven't you heard? Love conquers all."

He made a low sound of disbelief. "Sure it does, if you're Cinderella." He cupped her nape with his hand, loving the way silky strands curled around his fingers when he slid them through her hair.

"I believe in happy endings," she said, smiling up at him. "Don't you?"

He kissed her because he couldn't resist the temptation of her lips any more than he could refuse to draw his next breath. She went up on her tiptoes, her arms tightening around his neck. Her breasts were warm and soft against his

chest, and the scent of her perfume filled his nostrils. He
drew her up against him, one hand curving over her buttocks, molding their bodies together from shoulder to thigh.

He kissed her until he wanted more than kisses, and then
drew back. "Cinderella wouldn't have had such a happy
ending if she'd married a pauper instead of a prince."

Cindy punched him on the arm. "You're not a pauper!"

He made a broad gesture that encompassed the house and
the grounds beyond. "I am compared to all this."

She blew out a sigh of exasperation. "Come on, Pauper,
let's go get some breakfast. I'm starving."

He regarded her quizzically. "I didn't know you could
cook."

She made a face at him. "I can't," she said, taking him
by the hand. "Come on."

They didn't eat in the kitchen or the dining room, but in
something she called the breakfast room. It was located on
the east side of the house. The furniture was dark, the chairs
upholstered in burgundy velvet. One wall was mostly windows, offering a clear view of the morning sun and the yard.
There was an abstract painting on the opposite wall.

The maid who served them wore a gray uniform. She
appeared to be in her mid-fifties, making him think she'd
probably been with the family for a good many years. She
looked at him with barely concealed surprise, obviously
somewhat taken aback at finding a stranger at the breakfast
table. She recovered quickly and laid out a breakfast fit for
a king, asked if there would be anything else, and left the
room.

Ethan glanced at the bounty spread before them. Cindy
had told the maid to bring "the usual."

He looked at Cindy. "You eat like this every day?"

"Well, I don't. But my mom and dad can never agree on
what to have for breakfast, so the cook just makes a little
of everything and the help eats whatever is left over."

Breakfast was practically a seven-course meal. Orange juice, coffee, eggs—poached, scrambled, fried and over easy—bacon, hash browns, strawberry waffles, a basket of rolls and muffins, a plate of pastries. The table was laid with gleaming silver and delicate plates with a flowered pattern around the edges. The glassware was crystal.

"Where's the rest of your family?" he asked.

"Probably still asleep. It's not even eight yet."

"Yeah. What are you doing up so early?"

"I heard you moving around and thought you might be hungry, or at least in need of caffeine."

Regarding her over his coffee cup, he nodded. "Good call. What's your mother going to say when she finds out I spent the night here?"

"I don't know. I know Joe won't like it, but I don't think my mother will care. She always liked you."

He raised one eyebrow.

"Well, not in the beginning maybe," Cindy allowed. "How long can you stay?"

He shrugged. "As long as you need me."

She smiled at him, and it went straight to his heart. "Then you'll never go home."

He started to reach for her hand, then drew back when the maid entered the room. "Will there be anything else, Miss Cindy? More coffee?"

"More coffee sounds good. Do you want anything else, Ethan?"

He shook his head.

"Just coffee then, Adele."

The maid nodded and left the room.

A few moments later, Joe entered the room. He paused in midstride, his eyes narrowing when he saw Ethan at the table. "What's he doing here?" He spoke to Cindy, but his eyes remained on Ethan.

"He's here at my invitation," she replied coolly.

"Does Mother know?" Joe asked.

"Of course Mother knows," Claire Wagner said.

Cindy and her brother both turned as their mother stepped into the room.

Ethan started to rise, but Claire waved him off as she took a seat beside Cindy. "Sit down, Joe, and stop acting like an ill-bred bore."

Joe did as he was told, his expression mutinous.

"How are you feeling, Mom?" Cindy asked.

"Better. The hospital just called. They're going to move your father into a private room this morning."

"That's wonderful." Cindy took her mother's hand in hers and gave it a squeeze. "I told you he'd be all right."

"Yes, you did." Claire looked across the table at Ethan. "It's been a long time," she said.

He nodded.

She gazed at him through eyes much like her daughter's. "You're looking well."

"Must be that big breakfast I just ate."

Claire smiled. "Yes, Maricela is a whiz in the kitchen." She glanced at the covered dishes in the center of the table. "Did you leave anything for the rest of us?"

He glanced at Cindy before replying. "Not much. We don't get meals like this on the rez."

Claire laughed softly.

Joe glared at him.

"How long will you be in town, Ethan?" Claire asked.

"As long as Cindy wants me to be."

Claire's gaze rested briefly on her daughter's face. "I see."

"You needn't worry. I'll be staying at my mother's place."

"You're welcome to stay here," Claire said, and then added, "At least until my husband comes home."

Ethan looked at Cindy's brother. "Thank you, Mrs. Wagner, but I don't think that's a good idea."

"Well, the invitation stands if you change your mind."

The maid came in then, bearing a tray laden with covered plates. She had no more than set them on the table than Joe's wife and kids breezed into the room.

Cindy caught Ethan's gaze. "What do you say we get out of here and give them some room?"

He nodded.

"Mom, I'm going to show Ethan the grounds. What time do you want to go to the hospital?"

"The doctor said we could see your father about ten."

"All right, we'll be ready." She kissed her mother on the cheek, then took Ethan's hand and they left the room.

As soon as they were outside, Cindy put her arms around him. "I'm dying for a kiss," she said with a saucy grin.

He lifted one brow. "Are you?"

"Definitely. I think I shall expire on the spot if you don't kiss me right now. You don't want that on your conscience, do you?"

"Hell, no," he muttered, and wrapping his arms around her waist, he kissed her until she was gasping for breath.

"I may just die anyway," she said, "but oh, what a way to go!"

She felt good in his arms, warm and soft. His body reacted the way it always did when he held her, and he drew her close. "See what you do to me?" he asked, his voice thick. "I'm the one who's dying here."

"Are you complaining?"

"Hurting," he said. "Hurting from wanting you."

She gazed up at him, her eyes brimming with so much love it made his heart ache. "I can stop the hurt."

"Cindy…" He buried his face in her hair, tempted for one moment to take what she offered, knowing he would hate himself for it.

"I'm crazy about you, you know," she whispered. "I guess I always have been."

He groaned softly. "Cindy, honey..."

"Don't start," she warned. "I don't want to hear about how you're not good enough for me, or any of that other nonsense that pours out of you when things start to get serious between us."

He lifted his head and looked deep into her eyes. "I'm afraid of letting you down. I don't want you to give up what you have here to be with me. I don't want to be sitting across the table from you years from now and have you hate me because I can't give you the kind of life you're used to."

"Ethan—"

"Hear me out. The ranch will be mine one day, but it'll never make me rich, not the way your old man is rich. I'll never be able to give you vacations in Europe, or buy you a new car every year—"

"It doesn't matter."

"Doesn't it?" He looked at the house and the acres that surrounded it, at the tennis court and the pool and the three-car garage. "Are you sure? You've seen where I live—a four-room cabin. Can you honestly tell me you'll be happy living there? Hell, my place isn't big enough to hold half your clothes."

She laughed softly. "Oh, Ethan, I think the question is can you handle living with me?"

It was a good question, one for which he had no answer. They'd both been careful to avoid the word *love*, though they'd tiptoed around it.

"We'll work it out somehow," he said. He smiled down at her. "If you can stand being married to a man who doesn't have anything, I guess I'll have to find a way to put up with a woman who has everything."

He just hoped he could, because he wasn't sure he could let her go now that he'd found her again.

Chapter Eighteen

An hour later, they were on their way to the hospital. Cindy's mother rode with Joe and his family. Jimmy and Ilsa followed in their BMW. Cindy rode with Ethan.

At the hospital, he stayed in the waiting room while the family went in to see Cindy's father. One thing was for sure—her father didn't need to see him. Just knowing Ethan was in the building would probably give her old man a relapse.

Ethan sat there for a few minutes, watching some silly soap opera on TV, and then went out to pace the hallway.

He'd been walking up and down for about twenty minutes when Paul VanDerHyde rounded the corner. He came to an abrupt halt when he saw Ethan, and the two men stared at each other across six feet of black and gray tile.

Paul wore a pair of brown wool slacks, a beige polo shirt and brown loafers. His hair was slicked back. He looked exactly like what he was, vain and rich.

"What are *you* doing here?" VanDerHyde asked. He looked Ethan up and down, a pinched expression on his face, as though he'd just found a worm in his salad.

"Waiting for my girl," Ethan replied, emphasizing the words *my girl*. "What are *you* doing here?"

Paul snorted contemptuously. "She's not *your* girl, and she never will be."

"Is that right? As I recall, she went home with me last night. Or should I say, I went home with her."

Paul's complexion went white and then a mottled red as each word struck its target, sharp and clean as an arrow. Head high, he swept past Ethan and disappeared into Jordan Wagner's room.

Ethan chuckled softly. "Bull's-eye," he muttered, and headed for the coffee machine at the end of the corridor.

Cindy looked up when Paul entered the room. His face was red, and he looked as if he'd swallowed something unpleasant. He said hello to her mother, who was sitting at her husband's side, holding his hand. He acknowledged the rest of the family. Joe was sitting across from his mother. Rising, he shook Paul's hand. Kim smiled and said how nice it was to see him again. The kids, intent on the show on the TV, ignored him.

Moving closer to the bed, Paul nodded at Jordan. "Mr. Wagner, you're looking a lot better than the last time I saw you."

"Thanks, son," Jordan said weakly. "I'm feeling a lot better, too."

Paul smiled at him. "You'll be out of here in no time."

Jordan nodded. He glanced from Paul to his daughter. "Have you two worked things out between you?"

"Not now, dear," Claire said. Leaning forward, she brushed a wisp of hair from his forehead.

Cindy looked at Paul, standing at her father's bedside as if he belonged there. For the first time in her life, she felt as though she was standing on the outside watching someone else's family. Her father had accepted her embrace when she first arrived. He had been glad to see her, she had no doubt about that, but he had been cool, the air between them strained with the memory of their last conversation.

She stood abruptly, feeling the need to get out of there, away from all of them.

Her mother looked up. "Where are you going, honey?"

"It's crowded in here. I thought I'd step outside for a few minutes."

Her mother nodded, a knowing expression on her face

Cindy moved to the bed and squeezed her father's arm. "I'll see you later, Dad."

He nodded, but didn't say anything until Paul started to leave, too, and then he grabbed hold of Paul's hand. "Stay."

Feeling jealous and relieved, Cindy left the room. Closing the door behind her, she stood there for a moment, taking slow deep breaths, and then she went in search of Ethan.

She found him at the end of the corridor, gazing out the window. Just looking at him made all her senses come alive. Her heart beat faster, her skin felt warmer, there were butterflies in her stomach. Ethan.

He must have seen her reflection in the glass for he turned slowly as she approached him. His gaze moved over her, and then he frowned. "What's wrong? Is your father…?"

"No, he's fine." She moved into his arms and rested her cheek against his chest.

His hand automatically stroked her hair. "What is it, darlin'? What's wrong?"

"I don't know how to explain it. I was sitting in there, looking around, and…" She shrugged. "I looked at my father and my brother and I suddenly felt like I didn't belong. I looked at them and they were strangers, all of them except my mother, and suddenly I had to find you." She wrapped her fingers around his arm, reassured by the familiar strength she felt there. "I listened to Joe talking about his business and how well it was doing, and I watched Kim's face and

I knew she was thinking she'd rather have less money and more of her husband's time. And I knew then that that was what my mother had tried to tell me on my wedding day, when she said Paul would never make me happy, that there was more to life than just the things money can buy, and..."

She looked up at him. "And I love you."

"Cindy!" His arm tightened around her.

"Let's get out of here," she said.

"Are you sure?"

"Yes. I need to get away from here for a little while."

"Okay by me," he said.

They were waiting for the elevator when Paul came up behind them. Cindy glanced at Ethan, then at Paul, and prayed the elevator would come soon.

"I can't believe this is what you left me for," Paul said, sneering. "The Marlboro Man on steroids."

"Paul," she said wearily. "Just let it go."

"Your father will probably disown you if you marry this creep. And then what will you do? Go live on the reservation like some squaw and produce a dozen little redskin brats?"

A muscle clenched in Ethan's jaw. "My people don't like the word *squaw*."

"Who cares?"

"Paul!" Cindy glanced around, aware of the nurse's station only a few yards away.

"I'll handle this." Slowly and deliberately, Ethan put Cindy behind him.

"My mother lived on the reservation. I think you owe her an apology. And Cindy, too."

"I don't care what you think," Paul said with a sneer. He grabbed Cindy, his fingers digging into her arm. "Tell him to get lost."

"Paul, let go! You're hurting me."

"Take your hand off of her," Ethan said, his voice deceptively mild.

"Mind your own business, you dirty redskin."

"She *is* my business," Ethan said, and without warning, he drove his fist into Paul's face.

Paul shrieked as blood spurted from his nose.

The elevator arrived and the doors slid open. Grabbing Cindy by the hand, Ethan stepped into the car and pulled her in after him.

"How could you?" she asked as the doors closed. "I think you broke his nose."

"He's lucky I didn't break his neck."

She stared at him a moment and then, as the tension flowed out of her, she began to laugh. "If we're going to have a dozen kids, we'd better get started."

He grinned down at her. "Are you proposing to me?"

"I guess so. Should I get down on one knee?"

"No. Should I?" His expression turned serious as he took both of her hands in his. "Will you marry me, Cindy?"

Her mouth formed a perfect O, but no sound emerged.

"Is that a yes?"

"Yes. Oh, yes! Do you mean it?"

"I mean it. I love you, Cindy. I never stopped."

She threw herself into his arms and he stumbled backward, his arms locking around her waist. "And I love you!"

"Easy, girl," he chided softly, but she wasn't listening. She was covering his face and neck with kisses.

He didn't realize the elevator had come to a stop or that the doors had opened until he heard a round of applause and catcalls. Peering over Cindy's shoulder, he saw a half dozen people standing in front of the elevator.

Taking Cindy by the hand, he made a slight bow, then they stepped out of the car and hurried through the lobby.

Ethan was laughing out loud by the time they reached the

truck. Pulling her into his arms, he kissed her again. "You did say yes, right?"

"Stop laughing!"

"Come on, you have to admit that was pretty funny."

"Not!"

"It will be. In twenty years, you'll be telling our twelve kids all about it."

That did make her laugh.

"Come on," he said, "let's go look for a ring."

Cindy could barely contain her excitement as they entered a jewelry store and sat down at a counter. A moment later, a clerk approached them.

"May I help you?" he asked.

"We'd like to see some engagement and wedding rings," Ethan said.

The clerk beamed at them. "Very good, sir. Are you interested in gold, white gold or platinum?"

Ethan looked at Cindy, one brow raised.

"I like white gold. What do you like?"

"That's fine with me."

Unlocking the glass case, the clerk pulled out a velvet-covered tray that held an assortment of diamond rings.

Ethan shook his head. "Not those."

Cindy tugged on his hand. "Ethan, those are fine."

"Not for you." He pointed to another section. "We'd like to see those."

"Are you sure, sir?"

A muscle twitched in Ethan's jaw. "I'm sure."

"Oh, Ethan," she breathed. "They're beautiful, but they must cost a fortune."

"It'll be a good investment," he said. "After all, you'll be wearing them for the rest of your life. Which ones do you like?"

She looked them over carefully, but there was no need. She'd known the set she wanted as soon as the man pulled the tray out of the case. The engagement ring had a diamond in the center that was large without being ostentatious and there were three smaller diamonds on each side. "This one."

"Excellent choice," the clerk said. "Would you like to try them on?"

"Oh, yes," she said, and held out her hand.

The clerk slipped the rings on her finger and pronounced them a perfect fit. The diamonds winked under the lights.

The clerk looked at Ethan. "Will you be taking them with you?"

Ethan nodded. Reaching for his wallet, he pulled out a credit card and handed it to the clerk.

"May I?" the clerk said, and removed the rings from her finger. Putting the tray back in the case, he locked it up and put the key in his pocket. "I'll just be a few minutes," he said, and disappeared into the back of the store.

Ethan looked at Cindy. "Don't worry," he said. "My credit's good."

"But it's so much money. Are you sure…?"

He covered her mouth with his fingertips. "I don't want to hear any more about it. I wouldn't buy them if I couldn't afford it." Of course, it meant that he'd have to put off buying that piece of land he'd been saving up for.

"All right."

The clerk returned ten minutes later. He handed Ethan his credit card and a small sack bearing the name of the store. "Thank you, Mr. Stormwalker," he said. "Please come back if you need anything else."

The clerk's voice was edged with a note of respect that had been missing before, Ethan noted, and figured it was because his credit card had been accepted.

With a nod, Ethan stood up. He offered Cindy his hand and they left the store.

"I'd better get you back to the hospital," he said, "before your brother calls the cops."

She nodded. "I guess so." She slid her arm through his and they walked back to the truck.

The ball was over, she thought. It was time to get back to work.

Chapter Nineteen

The family was getting ready to go out to lunch when Cindy returned to her father's room.

"You're just in time," her mother said. She kissed Jordan on the cheek. "You get some rest now. We'll be back soon." Smiling, she linked her arm with Cindy's and they left the room, with Joe and his brood following behind. "Where would you like to go for lunch?"

"I don't care," Cindy replied, "as long as Ethan's welcome to come with us."

"Mother, I don't think—"

"Joe, I know what you think." Claire stopped and turned to face her son. "And I think you'd better get used to the idea of having Ethan around."

Joe stared at his mother and then at Cindy. "You aren't...don't tell me..." He raked a hand through his hair. "You're not going to marry that guy?"

"Yes," she said. "I am."

"Dad will never..." Joe shook his head. "It's your funeral. Sorry, Mother," he said. "Poor choice of words, all things considered. If no one has any objections, the kids want to go to the Burger Barn for lunch.''

"Fine with me," Cindy said. She smiled as they rounded the corner and she saw Ethan.

He saw her at the same time. He smiled, and then frowned when he saw Joe and his family trailing in her wake.

"Hi," she said. "We're going out to lunch."

He looked at her, one brow raised. "We?"

"All of us," she said, taking his hand. "Come on."

Ethan looked at Cindy's mother, awaiting her approval.

"All of us," Claire said. "That means you, too."

"It wasn't so bad, was it?" Cindy asked.

They were sitting in the gazebo with their arms wrapped around each other. Her mother and the rest of the family had gone to bed a couple of hours ago, but Cindy was too keyed up to go to bed. She didn't want to waste time sleeping, not when she could be with Ethan.

"Bad's a relative term, I guess," he replied.

"And my relatives are bad—is that what you're saying?"

He grinned at her. "Your mother's all right, but that brother of yours..." Ethan shook his head. "The word *anal* comes to mind."

"He's not so bad, just a little snooty."

"Uh-huh. At least Lance likes me."

Cindy smiled. When it came to Ethan, Lance had a severe case of hero worship. "Maybe we could invite him to the ranch next summer," she suggested. "I know he'd love it."

"Sure."

She snuggled closer, overcome by a sense of utter peace and happiness. They sat there for a time, content to be quietly close.

"Ethan?"

"Hmm?"

"Would you dance for me?"

"Here? Now?"

"Here. Now. Just for me." Sensing he was about to refuse, she said, "Please?"

"I think you should dance for me."

She felt herself blush, as she always did, whenever he suggested such a thing. She wanted to dance for him, had thought of it often, but she could never quite summon the nerve. "I will," she said. "Someday I will."

With a shake of his head, he stood and stripped off his shirt and T-shirt. He stood there a moment, and then he began to dance.

She leaned forward, her gaze never leaving him as he danced for her under the light of the moon. There were no words, no music, yet she knew he was telling her how much he loved her, that he was offering her his whole heart and soul, promising her that he would love her and cherish her not only for this life but into the eternities beyond.

There were tears in her eyes when he finished. He stood there a moment, his dark eyes intent upon her face, and then, kneeling in front of her, he took her hand in his.

"I love you, Cindy. Will you be my wife?"

"Oh, yes."

Reaching into his pocket, he withdrew a small velvet box and opened it, then slipped the engagement ring on her finger. "I'll try to make you happy so long as I live," he said fervently. "From this day on, I will live and die just for you."

She didn't know what to say, wasn't sure if, at that moment, she was capable of coherent speech. Tears filled her eyes, overflowing from the depths of a heart filled with love.

Gazing into her eyes, he drew her down into his lap and sealed his words upon her soul with a kiss.

They announced their engagement during breakfast the following morning. Cindy's mother accepted the news of their engagement with a smile and a tear. "I think I always knew you would end up together," she said, hugging first Cindy and then Ethan. "There was always a special glow in her eyes when she looked at you, a warmth in her voice when she spoke your name. I hope you'll be very happy together."

Cindy kissed her mother's cheek. "Thank you, Mom."

"I'll do my best to make your daughter happy," Ethan said.

"I think you're doing that already," Claire said. "Just promise you'll come to visit us often."

"We will," Cindy said.

"Where do you plan to live?" Joe asked.

"Wherever Ethan wants to," Cindy said.

Her brother shook his head in disgust and left the room.

"I'm sorry," Kim said. "He can be a real pain in the..." She glanced at her kids, who were sitting on the floor playing Monopoly. "In the fanny." She hugged Cindy. "I hope you'll be happy, both of you."

"So." Claire resumed her seat. "Have you set the date?"

Cindy looked at Ethan. "No."

"It's up to you." He grinned at her. "The sooner the better, as far as I'm concerned."

"Me, too," Cindy agreed. "How about next week?"

"Next week!" Claire exclaimed. "We can't plan a wedding in a week. And what about your father? He might not be well enough to—" She broke off, her cheeks turning pink. "I'm sorry, it's up to you, of course. Whatever you decide will be fine with us."

Cindy bit down on her lower lip, then looked at her mother. "Do you think Dad will walk me down the aisle?"

"I don't know, honey. But I'm sure Lance will if your father won't."

Cindy looked at Ethan. "Maybe we should just elope."

"Whatever you want, darlin'."

"Well, I really would like a small church wedding. Just you and me and our families."

"Then that's what we'll do," Ethan said.

"Mom, will you talk to Dad?"

Claire gave her hand a squeeze. "Honey, I think that's something you'll have to do yourself."

"I don't think this is a good idea," Ethan said.

"You don't expect me to face him alone, do you?"

Ethan shifted his weight from one foot to the other. "I think it'll be better for his health if you go in alone. You know how he feels about me."

"All right," Cindy said. "Give me a kiss for luck."

"You'll need it." He kissed her soundly, turned her around to face the door and gave her a pat on her shapely behind. "Go get 'em, darlin'."

Taking a deep breath, Cindy opened the door to her father's room and stepped inside.

He was sitting up in bed, looking much better than he had in days. His color was good, some of the tubes and wires were gone, and he looked more like himself.

"Hi, Dad." She moved to stand beside the bed, her hands worrying the straps of her handbag. "How are you feeling?"

"Better." He glanced at the door. "Where's your mother?"

"She'll be here in a little while. I wanted to talk to you alone for a few minutes."

"Oh. About what? She's not sick, is she? All this worrying over me can't be doing her blood pressure any good."

"She's fine, Dad."

He grunted softly. "Have you heard from Paul?"

Cindy took a deep breath and let it out in a long slow sigh. "No." There was only one way to say it, and she said it in a rush. "I'm getting married, Dad, to Ethan Stormwalker, and I'd very much like for you to walk me down the aisle."

Her father stared at her, blinked and stared again. "You want my blessing to marry that Indian dancer?"

"Yes. I love you, Daddy. I want you to be there."

He cleared his throat, reached for a glass and took a drink of water. "I don't like it. I don't like any of it. He's not good enough for you. What has he got? Nothing."

"I love him."

He looked up at her, his eyes narrowed, and then he sighed. "You're my only daughter. Of course I'll be there. And if you need anything…money, anything…just—"

She threw her arms around his neck and kissed his cheek. "Thank you, Dad!" She kissed him again. "I've got to go tell Ethan, and I've a million things to do. I'll see you later. Bye, Daddy, I love you!"

Ethan didn't have to be a mind-reader to know what Cindy's old man had said. Her eyes were sparkling, her face glowing with happiness, when she left his room.

Caught up in her happiness, Ethan lifted her off the ground and swung her around, pleased that her father thought more of his daughter's happiness than carrying a grudge.

They set the date for the wedding that night, called to reserve the church the next morning, and then, to Cindy's dismay, Ethan told her he had to get back to the ranch.

"Will I see you again before the wedding?" she asked.

"Not unless you come to the ranch," he said. "We're booked solid the next couple of weeks." He brushed a kiss across the tip of her nose. "I'm sorry, darlin'."

She sighed heavily.

"You're sure about this, Cindy? Sure you want to marry me?"

"Of course I am! Why?"

"I guess I just can't believe you're willing to leave all this."

"It's just things, you know. Things aren't important. But you are."

He wrapped his arms around her and kissed her, a kiss meant to last until he saw her again.

Hand in hand, they walked to his truck.

"I'll see you at the church if not before," she said. "Don't be late."

One more lingering kiss, and he was gone.

The next two weeks passed quickly. Her mother had returned her old trousseau to the stores, and Cindy went out and bought a new one. Instead of cocktail dresses, she bought Western shirts and skirts and jeans. Instead of a fur coat, she bought a sheepskin jacket. Instead of high-heeled shoes, she bought sneakers and boots. And for her wedding night, she bought a gossamer white nightgown.

They ordered flowers. She bought a ring for Ethan. Cindy asked Kim to be her maid of honor. There wouldn't be any bridesmaids this time. Ethan called and asked Lance to be his best man. Her brother was thrilled and strutted around the house as though he had just won the lottery. In the midst of all these preparations, her father came home, looking almost as robust as he had before he got sick.

Ethan called her every night and they spent hours on the phone, daydreaming about their future, making plans for their honeymoon in Hawaii.

And suddenly it was the day of the wedding.

Cindy woke to the ringing of the phone beside her bed. "Hello," she said, yawning.

"What are you doing in bed? It's your wedding day."

"Ethan." She melted inside at the sound of his voice.

"Still love me?"

"More than ever." She rolled over on her stomach and

looked at the clock on the bedside table. "Just think, in eight hours and fifteen minutes, I'll be Mrs. Ethan Stormwalker."

He chuckled softly. "I'm counting the hours, too, darlin', believe me."

"Are you?"

"I love you, darlin'," he said, his voice husky. "See you soon. I'll be the nervous one in the rented tux."

Eight hours later, Cindy stood beside her father, her hand resting lightly on his arm. They had picked a rustic church set amid towering pines. Both of their families were there, along with a few close friends. Sally Whitefeather beamed at Cindy from a pew near the front.

Cindy smoothed a hand down the front of her gown. Her father had declared it a foolish extravagance to buy a new wedding dress when she had one that was still practically new, but Cindy and her mother had been so appalled at the notion of Cindy wearing the same gown that he hadn't said another word about it, or even asked what this one cost.

There were no second thoughts as her father walked her down the aisle. Cindy smiled happily at her mother and her brothers, and then fixed her gaze on Ethan. Other than the night they had gone dancing at the lodge, she had never seen him in anything but jeans and T-shirts or his dance costume. Now, seeing him in a tuxedo, with his long black hair swept away from his face, he was easily the sexiest, handsomest man she had ever seen, and she determined there and then that she would never let him out of her sight.

Ethan watched his bride walk down the aisle, her face radiant. She was a vision in a gown of white satin, an angel in the guise of a woman. Love swelled in his heart and he thanked all the gods, red and white, for giving him one more chance to find happiness with the only woman he had ever loved.

And then she was there, beside him. He gazed deep into

her eyes. There were no doubts there, only love that would last a lifetime.

"Who giveth this woman to be married to this man?"

Jordan Wagner cleared his throat. "Her mother and I do." He gave Cindy's hand a squeeze and placed it in Ethan's.

"I love you." She mouthed the words as Ethan's fingers closed around hers.

"I love you."

Lost in the love she saw in Ethan's eyes, she found it took all the concentration she could muster to listen to the solemn words that made her Ethan Stormwalker's wife. Beautiful words that bound her to the man of her dreams. Tears welled in her eyes as he repeated the vows that made him her husband, and then he was lifting her veil, taking her in his arms. He gazed down at her, his dark eyes filled with love and the promise of forever.

Her eyelids fluttered down, all else forgotten as he kissed her as her husband for the first time.

Ethan's arms tightened around her. She fit in them as though she had been sculpted for him, and he kissed her with all the love in his heart, unable to believe that she was his. His hands moved up her back, feeling the smooth satin of her gown, moving up her neck, his fingers delving into her hair.

She moaned softly when he took his lips from hers, so he kissed her again, might have kissed her forever if Lance hadn't whispered, sotto voce, "Geez, sis, come up for air, will ya?"

Cindy laughed and Ethan laughed with her.

"And now," the minister said, a smile in his voice, "I give you Mr. and Mrs. Ethan Stormwalker."

Their families and friends stood, applauding, and then

they all gathered around, eager to shower the bride and groom with hugs and good wishes.

Later that night, when a big white limo pulled up in front of the ranch office, the bride wasn't alone.

Chapter Twenty

Ethan carried his bride up the stairs and into his cabin. "Are you sure you wouldn't rather go to a hotel for the night?" he asked, kicking the door closed with his heel.

"No. I want us to spend our first night here. After all, this is where I found you again. Where we fell in love again."

"I never stopped loving you."

"Don't you want to put me down? I must be getting heavy."

He shook his head, then claimed her lips with his own. She felt good in his arms. Tonight, he felt like he could move mountains and leap tall buildings with a single bound.

He kissed her until they were both breathless, and then, very slowly, he lowered her to her feet, letting her body slide intimately against his.

"Did I tell you how very beautiful you are?" he murmured.

"Once or twice in the limo, but I wouldn't mind hearing it again."

"You're beautiful." He ran the tip of his forefinger over her lips.

Her heartbeat slowed, then sped up.

"So beautiful." His hand cupped her breast, his dark eyes smoldering.

"I've waited all my life for this moment," she whispered. "For this night."

He lowered his head and rained kisses along the curve of her throat. "I hope the reality lives up to your dreams."

"Oh, it will, I'm sure of it."

"I'll do my best."

"Ethan?"

He paused in the act of kissing the inside of her ear, stayed by the tremor in her voice. "What is it, darlin'?"

"Have you made love to many women?"

He lifted his head and gazed down into her eyes. "What kind of a question is that to ask now? Have you made love to many men?"

She shook her head, her eyes wide. "None."

A slow smile spread across his face. "None?"

She had told him she hadn't slept with Mr. Moneybags, and he'd admired her good sense. He had always known Cindy was a good girl; it was one of the things that had attracted him to her. Still, he'd figured that sometime in the last five years she would have experimented, just once.

"I never wanted anyone but you."

"Cindy!" Touched beyond measure, he swept her into his arms and carried her to the bed. He held her close, kissing her gently at first, and then with increasing passion as he undressed her, baring her beauty to his gaze, pleased beyond measure that no other man had seen her or touched her.

He caressed her until she was quivering in his arms, until she reached for him, warm and ready and unafraid.

Her nails raked his back as she writhed beneath him, her

breath fanning his face as little moans of pleasure rose in her throat. He moved slowly and carefully within her, afraid of hurting her, wanting this, her first time, to be everything she had ever dreamed of, as she was everything he had ever dreamed of.

She cried his name as pleasure rose and crested deep within her.

With a cry of his own, he followed her over the edge into ecstasy.

Later, holding her close, one hand stroking her hair, he renewed his vow to love her with all his heart, soul, mind and body for as long as he drew breath.

Tomorrow, they would catch a flight to Hawaii. They would walk along the white sandy beaches and swim in the clear blue ocean, buy souvenirs for their families, and in the evenings they would sit in some outdoor café and sip drinks that sported little paper umbrellas.

But for tonight, she was his, only his.

Murmuring her name, he gathered her into his arms once more, determined to make her every dream come true.

And later that night, she danced, just for him.

Epilogue

Elk Valley Dude Ranch
Six months later

Cindy sat on the steps watching Ethan put the big buckskin stallion through its paces. They were a magnificent sight, the proud horse and the proud man.

She never tired of watching them. The stallion moved effortlessly, guided by the pressure of Ethan's legs and the subtle shifting of his body.

Wolf came and plopped down beside her, and she absently stroked the big dog's head. The last six months had been the best, the happiest, the most exciting of her whole life. She loved living on the ranch. When they were busy, she helped Dorothea up at the office. Sometimes she went along on trail rides with Ethan. Sometimes she helped out in the dining room. And some days she just sat back and enjoyed the beauty around her. They had hired an architect to design a floor plan for a house of their own. It would be finished in another few months. She could see the chimney just beyond the trees.

A smile curved her lips as she placed her hand over her belly. They had a bet going as to which event would occur first—the birth of their son or the completion of the house.

Her mother was constantly sending them presents for the baby. Dorothea had offered to baby-sit anytime. Even her father was coming around. Just the week before he had sent her a dozen roses for her birthday, and a child-size baseball and bat for his grandson.

Cindy walked toward the corral as Ethan dismounted, then stood with both of her arms crossed over one of the rails while he stripped the rigging from the stallion. He dropped the saddle over the top rail, laid the blanket over the saddle, draped the bridle over the saddle horn, and then ducked under the bars and drew her into his arms.

"Hello, Wife," he said, nuzzling her neck.

"Hello, Husband."

"How's my son?"

"He's doing handsprings," she said. "And jumping on the bed."

Ethan grinned at her. "Why should he have all the fun?" he said, taking her by the hand. "Come on, let's go inside and do some handsprings of our own."

"Best offer I've had all day." She squealed when he swung her into his arms and carried her up the stairs and into the house.

Cindy kicked the door shut with the toe of her boot. As Ethan carried her toward the bedroom, she glanced around the cabin that had been her home for the last six months. The place lacked many of the creature comforts she had once taken for granted. For a moment, she thought about her parents' house and everything she had left behind, and then she wrapped her arms around Ethan's neck and thought how amazing it was to think she had found everything she had ever wanted, everything she had ever needed, in a rustic four-room cabin in the wilds of Montana.

Smiling, she rested her head on her husband's shoulder as he carried her into the bedroom and shut the door.

*   *   *   *   *

*Madeline Baker creates another thrilling
Lakota hero in "Wolf Dreamer," part of*

Lakota Legacy

coming this summer from Silhouette Books